Finding the Real Road

Leigh Lincoln

This is a work of fiction. Names, characters, organizations, places, events, and incidents are either products of the author's imagination or are used fictitiously. Any resemblance to actual persons, living or dead, or actual events is purely coincidental.

Text copyright © 2021 by Leigh Lincoln All rights reserved.

No part of this book may be reproduced, or stored in a retrieval system, or transmitted in any form or by any means, electronic, mechanical, photocopying, recording, or otherwise, without express written permission of the author.

Please subscribe to my newsletter at
https://dl.bookfunnel.com/w9a91dyc7x
I'll send you an exclusive short story only for my readers.

I hate typos too but sometimes they slip through. Please send any errors you find to me; I'll get them fixed ASAP. I'm very grateful to eagle-eyed readers who take the time to contact me!
mailto:leighlincolnauthor@gmail.com

Chapter 1

As I stepped off the bus, the bright afternoon sunlight hit me. Blaring noises came at me from every direction, making my ears ring. The smell of grit and grime overwhelmed me, making my eyes water and my nose run. A blanket of heat and humidity tried to smother me. Nothing but the sight of chaos all around, and my heart sank to my toes as my whole body started to sway like a dandelion blown by a child. Pieces of my body began to shatter, left to drift on the gentle breeze.

I've made a mistake. A monster mistake. Amy, what were you thinking?!

My stomach swirled, I wanted nothing more than to turn around and climb right back on the Greyhound bus and return to my tiny, remote corner of the world. Go back to the place I'd once called home. In one hand, I clutched my backpack, my fist tighter on it than if it was a life preserver. The other waved around trying to grasp onto something, needing anything steady to cling to before I fell over.

A deep, smooth voice from behind me broke into my thoughts. "Miss? You alright? You need help?" To reassure me a smidgen, a hand gave a gentle squeeze on my elbow.

Turning my head a fraction, I saw the bus driver's concerned face. The ebony skin pulled tight across his high cheekbones. His dark eyebrows drawn down. His lips pursed.

"Yes, sir." My head gave a little shake, not sure in the least which of his questions I answered in the affirmative.

I didn't want to admit everything was far from fine. And that I needed aid. I'm too proud to let anyone ever see an ounce of weakness in me. Plus, nobody had called me 'Miss' in forever. Heavens, I was almost old enough to be his mother.

"Just tired from the long trip is all." Giving him a faint smile, I patted his sturdy hand.

"You're not from here, right?" He tipped his head to gain a better look at me.

"No, sir." This simple phrase couldn't come close to describing how far from home I had landed.

"Well, let's grab those suitcases of yours from the luggage cart, and then I'll find you a taxi. Sound like a plan?" His grip tightened on my arm as he ushered me off to the side a little way, out of the line of fire from the few stragglers still disembarking.

"Fine." I sighed in defeat, deflating quicker than a balloon with a hole in it. He wasn't going to let me leave this forsaken place. Oh, but there wasn't any way he'd ever understand why I wanted to. Why this alien world, with every pound of the jackhammer and toot of a horn, was killing me.

All of those hours on the bus, as mile after mile had passed, I'd been alone and wrestling with my thoughts. What I had run from. What I'd lost. What I'd abandoned. What I'd tossed aside. What I needed the most. Oh, I'm aware most people think everything revolved around the almighty dollar. But it's not like I had a money problem. No, there were much bigger issues in my life right then. Thus, I couldn't do anything but continue down this road I journeyed on. Because in so many ways this path wasn't going forward at all, rather it was leading me to a beginning of sorts. Or so I hoped.

Thus, here I now stood, or well, to be more precise, wobbled. A million miles away from everything I'd ever known. Doing something I shouldn't be doing. Trying to be someone I wasn't.

And lying to myself about how wonderful this all would turn out. Because, deep down, my bones told me, I couldn't run from myself or my problems. And thinking otherwise was nothing but pure foolishness.

I forced myself not to limp from leg cramps and the leftover stiffness of sitting for days. And then followed the driver to the baggage pickup area where I pointed to my two enormous cases. He snagged them, and we walked into the station.

"Sit here a minute. I'll return in a jiff; the office is in the back." He patted my shoulder with care as he lowered me onto a hard bench like I was a china teacup. He placed my belongings next to me before he strode off, leaving me to stare at the myriad of people milling about.

Old, young, fat, skinny, dirty, clean, whatever. Too many people to worry about, too many hours of me being awake, and too few seconds I'd be in this spot to make any difference. Yet, this used to be the type of place I'd hang out to find people who needed a hand up, not a handout. No longer.

And today was the worst day to have arrived somewhere new. This was a significant date, a day I should celebrate with someone important. With the person who meant the most in the world to me. However, for the second year in a row, I remained alone. Wondering if he was alright, if he missed me, and if his heart had been broken yet.

Before I melted into a puddle of tears, I whipped out my phone and pulled up his icon in my contacts. What do I say? Do I still have the right to call him "son?" Not exactly, not after what I'd said, what I'd done. Tapping my fingers on the screen for a moment, I almost chickened out. But this was important; he needed to understand I still cared. No matter what else had happed that hadn't changed. I typed, "Happy Birthday" and added a little cake emoji beside it. Then I hit send before I changed my mind. Lame, I know.

He's fourteen today, almost grown. And has lived with those people for over a year now. I squeezed the phone for a second, debating if I dared to take a quick peek at a few old photos. Oh, goodness, that would be way too much for me to handle. I'd sent him a quick note when I'd made my rash decision to move, hoping beyond hope he'd answer. Telling him where I planned to go, that I would always be there for him, and that he could call or text any time. I'd so wanted him to reply. To beg me not to leave him or plead with me to take him with me to this new place. Nothing. Radio silence as it had been since the day I dropped him off.

A few minutes later, the bus driver returned. Still, I clutched my phone, waiting for a ding saying I'd received a response. To be honest, no way there would ever be one. Not after all this time, all the harsh words we'd said. I shoved my phone in my pack like I'd been caught cheating in school, my face burning.

"I've got a cab waiting outside for you, okay?" Without stopping to ensure my agreement, he began picking up my luggage again.

Not saying a word, I shuffled along behind him to a car waiting by the curb near the main entrance. Everything was too much to handle. My head throbbed, my whole body hurt, and my heart ached beyond measure. Expressing my feelings an impossibility, and no confidant in sight even if I could.

The lyrics, "I was born in a small town, and I can breathe in a small town, gonna die in this small town," kept running through my head, but the words of this song were no longer true. I'd thrown away everything and would now die in a city. Yup, I'd stepped way out of line, and I didn't want to even try to do what everyone expected of me anymore. So much more unforgivable than anything else I'd ever done in my life.

Over the years, those oh-so-many big and small sins I found myself always committing were fodder for so much disappointment and gossip. But what drove me to consider this drastic move in the first place? Those sins alone? No, not entirely. In fact, the answer was something much bigger.

I'd dared to dream of something more than being stuck in the same rut forever and had left my tiny cocoon of a world. And now I stood here suffocating. No way could I ever fix this mess I'd landed in. I should've learned my lesson the first time I'd tried something along these lines in my younger days. The grass is never greener - doesn't matter where you go.

Once I settled into the backseat of the cab, the young man behind the wheel asked, "Where to, ma'am?"

I stared at the back of his head as I gave him the address. Those simple little words directed him to a place I hoped and dreamed to transform into my new home. A house I'd bought sight unseen in what for all the world felt like another lifetime, but in fact, was only a short time ago. Yes, I'd seen a bad grainy photo or two of the structure in an ad. Nothing to give me a great idea of what I would walk into.

However, the words "handyman special" in the ad were all I needed to hear. I'd paid for the place in cash through an unquestioning real estate agent I'd found online. You gotta understand how grateful I was for that. I didn't want a grilling about anything.

"Do you know where that is?" My words as polite as possible. After all, this is a big city; he couldn't know every nook and cranny. This wasn't my opinion alone. Every demographical website known to man listed it among the top hundred cities in the country. And it was the only real city I'd ever been in for more than a minute. No, I didn't travel much, or to be frank, at all. I'm the very definition of a homebody.

"Uhm, lady..." He coughed and then started again, "Do *you* know where that is?" He began to tap on the steering wheel with his long, skinny fingers.

What a strange thing to ask. Why would I have a clue? My legs started to twitch as they often did when I'm nervous and upset. "No." My heart fluttered, and my throat closed around the word I'd managed to choke out.

"Maybe you want to go somewhere else?" He turned a tiny bit in the seat to gawk at me. His deep black eyes matched his hair, his skin as white as the proverbial ghost. The small bit of his t-shirt visible to me faded and worn. Hard to tell what color it had started as, dark blue or purple perhaps. This poor young man couldn't make much at this job. My heart cried out in pain for a man I'd just met. Every inch of me wanted to invite him home for a proper meal.

"I don't understand." I looked right into his eyes, trying to figure out why he acted this way. Did he question all of his passengers about their personal affairs? Okay, time to muster up what little courage might still be left in my tank. Taking in a deep breath, I huffed out, "I gave you the address of my house. The key was overnighted to me, no problem. Not like any of this is your business."

I squeezed my hands into tight little balls, and then breathed out a slow, measured lungful of air as I released my grip. Exhaustion filled me. I didn't want to have this argument. This man needed to take me where I asked, and I wanted him to do it quick before I passed out.

"I think it would, uhm...I think you would want to go to a motel first. Drop off your luggage, maybe? Then go to this address after a late lunch?" His finger scratched the corner of his eye. "Or tomorrow morning?"

Oh, I so didn't need this right now. Every inch of me began to melt into the seat. This man had somehow sensed my mistake. No, no more doubts. The only path for me lay here, at this house. "No, please take me where I asked to go." I almost wagged my finger at him and stopped myself in the nick of time. I didn't want to come off sounding like his mother.

He didn't say another word as he started to drive. I snuggled into the seat as we went further and further into the city. Past the tall office buildings of the downtown area. Past what could only be an industrial area with boxy buildings and semi-trucks galore. Past a strip mall, fast food places, well you get the idea. Amazing to think there might be more businesses in this town alone than in my entire home state.

At last, we arrived. He pulled to the curb by an abandoned building that sat in a sea of structures as decayed as the one I stared up at. The house stood on weak, wooden pillars which appeared to be sinking into the sandy soil. The front porch leaned to one side, one post bent and broken. The faded wooden siding in desperate need of a paint job. In addition, all the windows were boarded up with huge sheets of battered plywood. A jungle of weeds surrounded the entire property. They beat at the sides of the house in such a way that the walls appeared to shake. From my position in the car, I couldn't spot the roof, but it would surely leak under the lightest of sprinkles. The whole structure remained standing by some miracle, hanging on by a thread for some time by the looks of things.

And I'd pictured it exactly like this during those long hours I'd been riding across the country on that dumb bus.

Yup, "special" described it well.

Chapter 2

When one comes from nothing, there's nowhere to go but up. Hence, as I now stood before my glorious new house, I gapped in awe. Of a disaster. The cab driver had dumped my bags at my feet and fled to safer ground without ever asking for the fare. The house before me utter perfection, more so than I had ever hoped. Wave after wave of emotions flooded me. So many memories from my youth when my parents were still living, and so many thoughts about how people viewed me because of where I came from.

For years, if anyone had ever asked me about my childhood, I never said it was anything less than wonderful. How to explain those years? The wilds of a western ranch and seldom leaving those acres and acres my parents owned. That land had more buildings falling down than standing. Settlers had once tried to farm the area long before my parents ever set eyes on it. My father, with loving hands, had rebuilt one tiny cabin for his bride. A love nest hidden away from the world where the two of them could grow old together.

And then I came into the picture. I shot a gun and rode a horse before I ever walked. Or so the legend went. Oh, I'm well aware that I wasn't born in those olden times you read about in *Little House on the Prairie*. But as certain as I'm standing, my parents raised me like I was. Our house not much more than a miniature log cabin in the deep dark woods. No utilities, and almost everything made by hand. Faith and family were the end all and be all.

My mother was a happy housewife, you know, June Cleaver style. She baked fresh bread almost every morning in a wood stove. Plus, she made wonderful meals from scratch each day. She'd sit for hours in her rocking chair, knitting, sewing – whatever. Oh, and despite the cabin having no running water, one couldn't ever spot a speck of dirt anywhere. Nope, she found the time to clean that place from top to bottom every day. Beds were always made. Laundry tubs by the back door were in constant use, as was the clothesline in the yard. I have vivid memories of her humming as she worked, seeming to not have a care in the world.

In addition, my mother was the hostess of more than a few women's committees for church and various Bible studies over the years. In all she did, she was polished and graceful as her mother had taught her. Didn't matter how she chose to live, she still had more than a touch of socialite still in her. Dresses and high heels didn't appear out of place in a log cabin when she wore them. They were part of who she was.

My father was a woodsman. Yes, that's what it sounds like. He cut trees down and sold them. Simple as that. He'd be out in the forest all day, allowing my mother the space she needed to keep the perfect home. Before he left each morning, he'd make sure she had plenty of water and firewood for whatever chores she planned to do. She would make sure his jeans and flannel shirts didn't have any holes in them and provide a jacket because it might rain or snow. She'd give him a passionate kiss, hand him his lunch pail, and wave until he was out of sight. Normal, send your man off to the office behavior.

At night, after dinner, they'd sit together by the fire discussing scripture. They were a perfect match. Holding hands as they whispered in each other's ears in their rocking chairs side by side. Pure bliss. And I never once saw them argue about anything.

There were whispers of why we lived as we did: Amish, Mennonite, hippies who refused to change with the times. In the end, the why didn't matter. This is what made my parents happy – being one with the land, being one in body and spirit, and having nothing to worry about. Each day would begin with a prayer of thanks to the Lord for the blessing of life. And each evening would end with a prayer of thanks for another day well-lived.

So, yes, I often hunted, fished, chopped wood, baked bread, knitted, and did whatever other chores were needed. Some days I became my mother's helper. Others, I would follow my father around the property. This was our family.

But I had a side that didn't connect with our home life. A part of me craved knowledge of all those things beyond my tiny world. Therefore, I read every book anyone put into my hands – by candlelight more often than not. Science, math, history, foreign lands, you name it … I learned it all. My local library in the town up the road had to borrow books far and wide to quench my thirst for information back then.

My big adventures to the great beyond fueled part of this desire. Every few years, my parents sent me to visit my grandparents back east. Both sets lived in the same area, almost neighbors. But everyone agreed I would be more comfortable at the summer "cabin" that belonged to my grandparents, on my mother's side. To me, it was a mansion, a rambling place in the countryside with more rooms than I could count. Thus, I never did see the city they lived in, not even once. Fine by me. The summer home was overwhelming enough.

Grandparents, cousins, aunts, uncles, distant relatives would float in and out during my brief stays. I never did try to keep track of them all. My grandparents on my father's side died when I was rather young. I don't remember them much, to be honest. All those people from the other side of the country almost didn't feel like a part of my life. No, they were more of an obligation I had to fulfill to keep my parents happy.

However, during those trips, I learned my mother and her mother were two peas in a pod. They looked alike, acted alike, and dressed alike. But my grandmother made it clear she didn't agree with my mother's choice of lifestyle. She'd whisper things to me like, "You're going to end up with nothing, honey." Or she'd hint, "You don't want to be treated like trash, do you?" Or she'd say, "You need to learn to be a proper lady."

As a child, I didn't quite understand her words. Yet I could see she didn't treat me the same as her other grandchildren. My grandmother always placed me at the end of the table and served me last. Okay, I'm sure part of this was my fault. I played just as hard while there as I did at home, and her maid had a difficult time getting me cleaned up before dinner.

At home, until I became a teenager, I only had to wear a dress for church. The rest of the time my mother allowed me to wear my dirty jeans and ripped t-shirts. On the other hand, at my grandmother's, I had to wear a dress for dinner. And heaven help me if I spilled one drop of liquid or one crumb on the dumb thing while I ate. And during the day, my grandmother wanted me to wear slacks and a blouse. Which shouldn't ever have a speck of dirt on them. Not so easy to do while riding a horse or climbing a tree or whatever mischief I got up to while I visited the summer "cabin." A place where I quickly learned it was better to spend time with the paid help than the relatives.

My grandmother often questioned me about my mother, asking about things I couldn't answer. Once, she asked if my mother still played the piano. I'd shrugged and didn't give any reply. I'd never once seen my mother anywhere near a musical instrument much less play one. Strangely, my grandmother never once mentioned my father at all. To her, he didn't exist.

One other thing I learned about family dynamics: my grandmother tolerated my other set of grandparents but nothing more. The few times all my grandparents were at the same table for dinner, the room remained silent. Unless someone spoke with me, the remainder of the group shared nothing at all. Almost thankful that by the time I turned ten, only my grandmother on my mother's side remained living. So much easier that way. But she sold the "cabin" when I was eleven, ending my visits. Do believe I did a little dance when I heard about that.

Needless to say, my childhood was an interesting one.

Whether for good or bad, I grew into a strong-willed young lady, sure and tough as any man. However, it wasn't enough to allow me to live my own life. Oh no. My father made it clear the only way off the ranch was through marriage. Our family followed the rules, my father being a rather strict man who believed everything the church told him. Every Sunday, he took notes on the sermon and spent the next week memorizing them. He ended up become a walking hermeneutics textbook. Ask him any question about a Bible passage and he'd be more than happy to give you a detailed lesson on it.

Above all, my father made it clear that thoughts were as important as actions. He would often hold my hand in his as he looked up to the heavens. "Never forget, the Bible says, 'For as he thinks within himself, so he is.' Your heart and mind must always be pure, honey."

My mother had a different approach to gaining my conformity – guilt. She was a master at making me feel shame over every little thing I did. I always made my skirts too short because they were hitting my kneecaps, not my calves. My neck showed because I'd ripped off the top button of my blouse. My fingernails were chipped and had dirt beneath them because I'd forgotten to use the file. Don't get me wrong, she wasn't mean. Only making sure I stayed on the straight and very narrow path.

As a child, I didn't mind the discipline, the firm hand keeping me deeply rooted in faith. I obeyed almost without question. I loved God above all else. I honored and obeyed my parents. I tried not to wish for things I didn't have. I vowed to be faithful to only one man when the time came. I went to church every time the doors were opened – Sunday school, services, choir, youth group, you name it. I didn't lie, cheat, steal, or swear.

Nevertheless, the more I read and studied, the more I wanted to see what else was out there to be explored. No matter how much I loved our little corner of the woods, it wasn't enough to satisfy me. And this, I discovered from my parents, borderline coveted what my neighbors had. So, it was wrong. Yet, still, I hungered for more. My father warned me this was treading on a treacherous path. Simple was better.

I persisted in my desire to be on my own, but my father didn't agree. Out *there* was way too dangerous for a single woman, for a woman must be pure in all things. The job of a husband, on the other hand, was to make sure she stayed in that state of purity at all times. Women were nothing but helpmates, created to follow behind their men. My mother was a prime example of this. She never did anything but follow a step behind my father while she provided a cozy home for him.

Consequently, at the beginning of the summer I turned eighteen, I stood at the altar. Saying my vows to a boy I'd seen only once before. He was but a few years older than me. New in town from somewhere out in the great big world – or probably only the next county over. My parents had said he was a fitting match. I didn't disagree.

Because who he was didn't matter. What he was, did.

All I needed was a warm, breathing male to spring me out of my prison. Oh, I'm aware, I'm being way too dramatic about this. My parents' cozy home wasn't as bad as all of that. They did allow me to drive the ten miles into town almost anytime I wanted. Still, every baby bird needs to leave the nest and fly away. Build something for themselves.

But problems between my new husband and I began from the start. And I'm not talking the beginning of the marriage. Nope. I'm talking from the moment of our engagement. When he dictated all the terms of our future marriage in about ten seconds flat.

I walked into the little DQ that evening with its bright orange and pink décor and went straight to the only person in the place sitting alone. His dark hair cut short, not a hint of a five o'clock shadow on his face. He wore a bright white polo shirt and khakis. On the table, a basket of french fries and a cup of chocolate ice cream.

I put out my hand. "Hi, I'm Amy. And you must be Tom, right?"

"Hey, babe. This thing's gotta be done quick. Like next week. I've gotta head out of town again for, uhm, stuff, work, yeah, you know." He looked over his shoulder and out the window. "So, I don't care if it's all fancy or anything. The church should be free."

Hold up. I met this guy a minute ago and he wants to get married in a week? No preamble, no introductions, nothing? "Kinda short notice. Don't we want to wait a bit? Maybe have a few more dates?" His eyes were still staring outside. For the life of me, I couldn't figure out why.

"No point. This is meant to be, dear." His head did a slow crawl back toward the center of the room, but his eyes still weren't focusing on me. He grabbed a fry, dipped it in the ice cream, and munched on it. "Oh, and I bunk with some buddies when I'm in town. You know a place we can live? Nothing fancy. I'm not here much. I travel all the time, don't you know."

I put my elbows on the table, my chin on my hands, and gazed at the man who'd been picked out for me. Well, my parents decided to get married after sharing a single cup of coffee. Who was I to argue with what God wanted for my life?

"I can find one." I tried to look into his eyes. However, they were now pointed up toward the air vent.

"Oh, and we can't have a honeymoon. I can't get time off from, uhm, work, right. I just started, you know. I'll find us a motel for the night in another town near here." He tapped on the table with the ice cream cup. A glob plopped over the side, splashing onto the surface. He swirled his finger into it, making a wide mess. He played with the ice cream for a while. Was he trying to paint with it? Odd, but I was aware some people play with food. Just not in public.

On and on Tom went as we sat across each other at the local DQ. Becoming engaged over french fries dipped in chocolate ice cream. Weird didn't go far enough to describe the occasion. And it terrified me to speak up against the whole thing. Didn't matter the impression of how forced and rushed the whole thing appeared to be. Because all I needed to do to become an adult was to be married. Rules were made to be followed.

Chapter 3

The evening before the ceremony, I became so ill that standing was almost impossible. I spent the night hunkered over a bowl of steam, trying to clear my head. Which, might I add, wasn't the easiest thing to do. Not with me having to keep getting up and refilling the bowl from the huge pot on the woodstove. And then add wood to the fire. Or water to the pot from the rain barrel out back. Oh, the joys of living in a cabin with no creature comforts.

Yes, I could've alerted my mother to the circumstances. She and my father had set up a tent just down the hill. You know, to give me some privacy for the week before my wedding. However, as an almost married woman, I wanted to handle this situation on my own. Gigantic mistake. Not my first and not my last by far.

On the morning of my nuptials, my mother found me lying on the rough wood floor of the kitchen. Snuggled up in a knitted wrap on the woven rag rug before a cold stove. Covered in snot, drool and who knows what else, and beet red from my fever. "Oh honey, you can do better than this!" she declared after taking one glimpse at me.

"Uhm, grm..." I tried to mumble something, but the cotton in my mouth made speech incredibly difficult.

"You're whiter than the dress you've spent all week sewing. Do believe I should've helped you with that. Did you sleep at all in the last few days?" My mother struggled mighty hard to pull me through the house, into my room, and onto my bed. I was dead weight and unable to help in any way, shape, or form.

"Mmm..." I grunted in reply.

"Alright. Let's see what we can do about getting you to look at least a tad bit human," she answered as she brushed my matted hair out of my eyes with tender fingers.

To this day, I have no idea how long it took her to make me somewhat presentable. It couldn't have been a cinch with no running water. But my mother was a bit of a miracle worker, and it didn't take her long to get me in a more presentable state. Still, fixing my puffy face wasn't possible.

When we got to the church, I headed downstairs and straight toward the closest mirror. Didn't quite make it before a dizzy spell hit me hard and I almost plowed into the nearest wall. I heard whispering as I leaned onto the cold brick next to the door of the ladies' room. Mistakenly, I'd thought the gossip from everyone in there had to do with my less than perfect appearance.

"Drunk."

"Out all night."

"Can you believe it!"

No, I didn't believe any of it. My friends and at this moment, bridesmaids, should've known better than that. A hangover and the worst case of pneumonia ever don't appear the same. Not even a little bit, thank you very much. And then it hit me like a slap. It wasn't me they were going on about. They hadn't seen me yet. Someone else must be in the mix here. I so didn't want to start thinking about what that meant. This was my day; I was getting what I wanted – freedom. Happy thoughts only. Don't burst my bubble, please.

Still, right at that moment, I didn't have any more strength than a newborn kitten. Hence, mounting a defense or trying to figure out what was going on wasn't a possibility no matter how much I might have wanted to try. But I did need to stop chugging cold medicine like spring water because I had this sensation like being stuck in a fog thicker than my grandmother's porridge. So, I did the easiest thing. I pushed myself away from the wall and ignored everyone. Didn't go into the bathroom to fix my face as had been my plan. Nope, I spun around and went the other way.

I walked back into the room my father waited in and found him wearing a rather stern look. "Honey, you are getting married today."

At the time, I thought it was a rather odd thing to say, or rather an odd way to say it. A statement, not a question. Part of me wished to go back in time. Everything about this day felt wrong. "Why, Dad?" I plopped onto the nearest couch, and my dress whooshing around me. The beading caught the light, sending a rainbow of sparkles around the room.

"You made a commitment. You must always be a woman of your word. Most days, your word is all you'll have." He stood up, took a few strides to my side of the room. Sitting next to me, he took me in his big arms. "This is the man for you, the man chosen for you. Even in the Bible, sometimes marriages weren't always perfect but were part of God's plan." He squeezed me tight, kissing the top of my head. "God's plan is flawless, no matter what."

Okay, he had me there. Only a few months ago the pastor had given a month-long sermon series on Hosea. Talk about a train wreck of a relationship! The wife wound up being a lady of the evening and all. But why would my father want something like that for me? I looked up at his face, strong, solid, no emotions whatsoever.

Faith had to be the answer here. This had to be the right path for my feet to be on. Arranged marriages work all the time. Love grows with time. I'd read lots of books where this was the case at least. And no matter what, you just can't question God's judgment about anything. My father had told me, "It's God's will. Don't ask why," so many times in my life that I'd learned the best thing to do was just float. Let things come as they may and trust some kind of plan I wasn't privy to existed.

"Yes, sir." Yet, something deep inside nagged at me to jump off this merry-go-round. Before the spinning got out of control.

My father walked – rather, dragged – me up the steps to the main hall with my head on his shoulder and his arm around my waist. Then down the aisle we went to my waiting fiancé. Tom stood there, not turning back to look at us at all. As I drew near, I looked up at him to see if I could tell. Not if he loved me. I didn't care one iota about that. Rather, I tried to tell if he was drunk. But in the end, that didn't matter either. Again, the who wasn't important. The why wasn't as important, even. This had now become a matter of faith and doing what my faith required. Of being the woman my parents wanted me to be. There didn't appear to be any other choice. My father shifted my weight from his arms to Tom's, leaving me propped against my soon-to-be husband.

I don't remember the minister saying anything before Tom nudged me hard with his elbow. Lost in thought, I wondered if I was doing the right thing after all. Seemed like this was going to be more of a sacrifice than a gift. My life for my freedom. Kinda a big ask. My mind flitted back to those moments in the DQ, and how Tom wouldn't look at me directly. Not once during the whole time. Something about him didn't seem right, and my father had realized something I hadn't. Yet, somehow, my father remained firm that this marriage was supposed to be. In the blink of an eye, Tom hissed in my ear, "Say 'I do,' now!"

So much for the wedding bliss and fairytales every girl dreams of. He slid a ring on my finger as I said the words. We had now both said our vows before God and man. Tom gave me a little peck on the cheek, we turned to the claps of everyone in attendance. And walked out man and wife. How something so simple could be so life-altering I'll never understand.

After someone pulled me out of the chapel, I melted into the chair in the reception hall. I sat there, watching everyone have fun at a party in our honor. Tom leaned his elbows on the table, his face in his hands, and didn't participate much. I knew beyond any shadow of a doubt I must do my sacred duty. I'd been raised for this moment, for whatever this marriage would bring into my life. For better or for worse. The boiling in my gut told me nothing good could come out of this.

The honeymoon night wasn't any better. Most of the evening I leaned in a rather awkward position in Tom's truck in front of the pale blue house I'd rented for us. I tried to ignore my companion as I stared out a window with a bad tint job. There were bubbles everywhere bigger than my fist, making the whole world wavy and oddly shaped. Which was how I had begun to feel my life now was – off-kilter, never to be righted again.

The place was a cute little one-bedroom house, with a white picket fence around the yard. I'd put a few things in there the day before the wedding, prepping it for us. I would've offered to have Tom do the same, but I didn't know how to call him. However, furniture and clothing weren't my problem at the moment.

We didn't leave town at all. We stayed parked in that same spot for way longer than we needed to. Most of the time spent in silence as we fumed at each other. So, no, definitely not a honeymoon.

Tom eased the truck to the curb, turning the engine off. Rotating in the seat, his right leg twisted and his knee ended up just behind the gearshift. "This is the right address, Amy, yes?" He rotated his fist on his thigh.

"Yes, isn't it adorable?" I twirled a curl that'd come out of my updo, nervous to be with a man alone for the first time in my life.

"No, it's all wrong." He looked past me at other houses on the street.

"Oh, why?" My face hurt from trying to keep the smile on.

"It's blue!" he barked at me. He reached over and started to shake me like a rag doll. His face purple with rage, veins popping out everywhere. "Blue!" He released me, banging on the dash.

I attempted to orient myself, while the whole world spun sideways. "Uhm, yes." *What have I done to make him so mad?* My hand reached out for the door handle. He stretched out across the cab and slapped it. I pulled my whole body into as tight a ball as I could for a brief second.

Every inch of him looked like it twitched, pulling and tugging. His fingers danced on his leg. His eyes darted from object to object outside the truck, every once in a while switching back toward me. I had no idea what I should do right at that minute. But my own rage started to build. How dare he swat at my hand! I glared at him for a while, but that didn't get me anywhere. Shifting my gaze toward the house, my heart yearned for something more. I so wanted to find some freedom in that place. And now I was trapped in a truck with an angry man. No, I was stuck with my husband.

His fingers began to pound out a rhythm on the dash. I pretended I didn't hear a thing. Don't ask how long this went on, but the shadows had gotten much longer. The cadence stopped, and he cleared his throat. With more than a little bit of hesitation, I turned my head toward him again.

"Go on, get out." He waved his hand at me, dismissing me like a child.

As sluggish as a sloth, I pried open the door and began to crawl out of the truck. The best thing I could do at that junction – well, the only thing – move slow. Half afraid of what he might do next.

Not waiting for me to close the truck door behind me or even to take my hand off the handle, he pressed on the gas, tearing off like a shot down the street. Tilting to the side at a dangerous angle, I grabbed one of the pickets of the fence as I observed the open truck door flop for a moment. I guess the speed of the vehicle slammed it shut at some point because the movement stopped as Tom careened around the corner. Somehow, I managed to keep myself upright long enough to enter the house before passing out for hours.

Must say, when I woke up, it was a mite odd being somewhere other than my parents' tiny cabin. This place smelled funny, like bread gone stale. Everything shone way too bright under the harsh artificial lights. Plus, I loathed beyond measure how loud the toilet was. The thing sounded like it gurgled whether I used it or not. Nothing like my grandparents' "cabin." Or maybe I just didn't notice things so much as child.

Please, just let me go back to the peace and quiet of my woods. Well, not so quiet. I missed the cry of the birds and the singing of the wind. Here there was nothing to listen to but the weird sounds of the house and the loud cars on the street.

However, this was the biggest part of the deal with marriage: the outside world. What I'd wanted most of all. To live in town with the "real" folks and have all the creature comforts. Thus, I was going to make the best of it. But cooking on an electric stove wasn't easy. In fact, it turned out to be far more difficult than cooking on my mother's old wood-burning stove. So glad Tom didn't come back to eat the burnt mac and cheese I'd attempted to make for dinner. In the back of my mind, some little part nagged at me that his quick getaway wasn't because he needed to return to work.

Still, I ignored those feelings. Instead, I took the giant leap of faith and trusted my new husband. He traveled a lot for work, so something must've come up. Leaving on the day of our wedding wasn't ideal, but sure, okay, he was providing for us. Uhm, he'd said he traveled a lot but not in the exact same sentence as he said he worked. Still and all, I wasn't going to quibble about this bit of weirdness. Not after the incident in the truck.

This adjustment to my new world and reality wasn't going to be as simple as I'd imagined. Almost felt grateful for the time to myself as I got my bearings. Being alone allowed me to sleep in the backyard under the stars rather than in the bedroom. To cook on a campfire, to bathe using the garden hose – yikes, I'm not going to go on. Odd behavior, I understand. But, at first, this comforted me more until I got a bit used to the new-fangled gadgets in the rental house. You know, like the toilet, sink, shower, and stove. Yup, I didn't use those things often when I visited my grandparents either. Don't ask about the awkward moments when I'd been caught in the woods as a child trying to do my business. I couldn't find an outhouse anywhere, so what was I supposed to do? Moving on.

A few days later, I was almost over being sick, and I waltzed into the local coffee shop to get a hit of caffeine and beg for a job. Because, yeah, you guessed it, Tom hadn't come back, and he hadn't left me any money. I felt too embarrassed to ask my parents what had happened to the money tree from the wedding meant to help us start our new life on the right foot. It had vanished without a trace.

The first person to pop up on my radar – my friend Wendy. Cringing inwardly at the sight of her wave, I wanted to turn around and run. She'd been one of my bridesmaids who'd said those unkind things right before my wedding. I knew her voice so well; we'd been friends forever.

Of course, this is how my luck always ran. Didn't matter where in town I went, one of my so-called friends was bound to show up and say something. Who was I kidding? This burg wasn't big enough to hide a flea in.

"Hi, hon." Wendy drew close, with her perfect everything... dress, hair, and makeup. "I so hoped you were okay after what happened and all." Giving me a swift squeeze, she patted my arm as she showed me a faint smile.

Uhm, back up. *What in the world is she talking about?* Flustered, I made the only response to leap into my head, "Getting better." I gave her a slight amused smirk in return. Fake it until you make it, right?

"Bless your heart. I mean, who does that, right? Goes out drinking all night right before they get married? And when my

Steve found him, well, let's just say the bimbo he'd attached himself at the hip to should be arrested." She gave a light chuckle. "And only a few minutes before he was supposed to be at the church. Still don't know how the guys got him cleaned up enough to get him in front of the minister. And so fast too. Wow, a real miracle that." Her eyes rolled up to the ceiling, thanking God for this act of kindness He'd given.

But God and His mercy weren't where my mind went. Nope. I screamed to myself, *Wait, what?! It had been Tom who'd been drunk? And he'd gone out all night with a floozy? And now he'd gone missing? Sugar, what am I supposed to do with this news?* Yeah, certain info should've been shared with me before I'd made a vow to this man. Not after. Now I'm stuck. As in till death do us part, trapped forever, stuck. *Was this what my father hinted at before the ceremony? Had he known all about this mess?*

Mainly because I didn't have a clue as to what else to do, I stood there frozen. Divorce is a sin, as in huge, never-to-be-forgiven sin. I had no idea if annulment is one as well, but at that point, there wasn't anyone I was willing to ask. My parents had raised me believing in the sanctity of marriage. A woman's purity the end-all, be-all. She wasn't getting into heaven without it. Marriage wasn't a thing one can toss aside like an old shoe. Add to that my father's conviction that marriage was part of God's plan for my life. And all of these things were not matters one discussed in the public forum. I needed to shut this conversation down, and right quick at that.

Good grief, my marriage was what – a day or two old, right? How does one count these things when the husband went missing? This wasn't happening. I wanted to slap myself silly. Oh, my heavens, what was I supposed to say in response to this bombshell? Well, doing something my mama would be proud of seemed my best bet. Just ignore the pain grinding in my gut and the migraine coming on. And pretend the world was my oyster, nothing was wrong in my life.

I said in a rush, "Oh, my, he was blowing off steam as boys will do, you know. He was just fine at the wedding; you know that as well as I do. Everything's perfect. We're doing wonderful. Thanks so much for asking." I plastered on the biggest fake smile you ever did see. Grinding my teeth into dust as I did, my jaw screamed in agony.

And I continued to show the phony grin for days, weeks, and months. Much easier than anything else I could've done. Nobody wanted to hear me howling from dawn till dusk. Oh, the insanity of it all.

Turned out to be no problem to convince Bob to give me a job that morning in the coffee shop once Wendy had left me alone. He'd known me since the day I was born, well almost.

So, as far as money was concerned, I'd set myself up. However, everything else in my life started rolling downhill into a total disaster. There were those funny looks everywhere I went. You know the ones. People take one little peep at you and then are quick to turn their eyes to anything or anywhere else. Oftentimes, people would rush across the street as I drew near. Oh, I knew it was so they could keep talking about me without me overhearing the dirty details. But through it all, my determination to keep my head held high and pretend the world wasn't burning to the ground remained strong. No problems in my life at all.

Therefore, as I moved around my little town, I had a beam on my face from ear to ear. And it grew large enough to brighten the darkest soul's day. Didn't matter if I worked long hours in the coffee shop, went about town doing an errand or two, or tried in vain to ignore the gossip. My face shone like the noonday sun.

Though, as the song says, "But I know the neighborhood, and talk is cheaper when the story is good, and the tales grow taller on down the line."

Yeah, I stuck out like a sore thumb with all those wagging tongues. A small town of something like a hundred people was no place to hide anything. Everyone noticed my husband had gone AWOL. There wasn't any way possible to have a job where you never came home. As in not once all summer long. These wonderful people kept each other informed about what I had for breakfast, lunch, and dinner for pity's sake. And the tales of my activities were whoppers from the snippets I overheard.

Chapter 4

Therefore, when a few months after our nuptials Tom still hadn't popped back in to say hi, I moved to the big city. Well, what one considers to be a large town in a state with almost no one. The place had less than five thousand people. But, to me, it was big enough to become lost in.

I bought a little old, beat-up Volkswagen Bug with my savings and moved all by my lonesome. Determined to make something of myself, I enrolled in college. Not caring in the least if Tom followed me. Or where he'd been since he'd dropped me off after our non-existent honeymoon. Or where he was right at that moment in time or, well, any given moment for that matter.

In those months of my so-called marriage, I got rather amazing at ducking questions. This is when the rain from my lies began to create a very slippery slope for me and when I started picking up speed on that downhill slide toward unbelief.

Because it appeared to me that my married life wasn't different from my single life except for sin. Now I stood on rather dangerous ground as far a sin went, I walked on eggshells everywhere. For a sin of omission is as bad as one of commission, after all. And I wasn't letting anything escape out of my lips about Tom. Yup, so far, my guilt consisted of out-and-out lying, anger, coveting, not going to church every time the doors were open, and not being as truthful as I should've been. Other items might've been on the list. I think after a while I stopped ticking the boxes off in my head.

Honest, only one thing changed. I now got up in my tiny rental house alone. I ate a quick breakfast alone. I went to work alone. I came home, ate a late-night dinner, dropped into bed, and slept alone. Waiting for a husband who I had no idea if or when would show back up. Or if he was a real living breathing human being. Yep, I went from living with my parents to living with the ghost of husband present.

Oh, sure, I still showed up at church sometimes. Always made my entrance after the music had started so I could slip into the back row. And of course, I left during the closing hymn. Don't get me wrong; my problem wasn't with God. Or with my parents, exactly. No, my faith that God had a divine plan for my life remained very much intact despite everything. I'd listen to the sermon with such intent, hoping to hear a word from the Lord at what I should be doing. Some clue as to what my next move should be.

However, at the same time, those church biddies and their gossip were making my life a living nightmare. Every time they left a message on my answering machine of "We're praying for you two tonight at the prayer circle. Can you call back with your specific requests?" all I could do was cringe. Or cry. Or scream. Or all of the above at once. Because I knew all they were doing was fishing for info for the rumor mill.

Still, my faith that God would fix everything wrong in my life kept me going. For a while at least. 'Now faith is the certainty of things hoped for, a proof of things not seen.' Oh boy, how I hoped and wished for so much. Most of all, I only wanted everyone to leave me alone for five seconds. But beyond that, I needed to see where this path He'd placed me on was going. I longed for some proof that I'd, in fact, done the right thing by doing what my father had told me to do. Though, no giant light ever seemed to shine on my path.

And at some point during this time of waiting, I decided enough was enough. My father and the church had been wrong, and I'd been right all along. I was more than capable of conquering the world on my own. Thus, I fled to what appeared to be a way out of the mess: college. I'd earn a degree and move on to bigger and better things. And, no, I didn't consult with my parents about any of it. They'd help me land in this muddle after all. Purity is a state of mind, not of body alone. I wasn't going to give even a peep at or be anywhere near a man for the rest of my life. I had no desire to repeat my one experience with a man.

But as a strong woman of faith, who obeyed God and her parents without question, the perfect candidate to become a pastor could be none other than me. I felt this so strongly that I came to the conclusion the reason the marriage had been allowed to happen had to be this. To test my level of obedience. And I'd passed with flying colors.

On the day I left for college, I told my parents where I planned to go, that I'd be back for break, and that I'd write often and not to worry. I lied and said Tom had a new job there. We were going to be great. Life was moving on.

***

Shaking my head as a song floated into my mind, "The memories are time that you borrow to spend when you get to tomorrow... collect the dreams you dream today." All I'd ever had were dreams that I'd never acted on. Or not fully enough to bring them to fruition.

Something else hit me as I planted my feet before my new home in this new town. All these years later, I'd done the exact same thing. After I'd landed in another giant disaster created by Tom, I'd upped and moved to a new place alone, simple as that. Making my own rules, doing what I wanted, and not caring in the least what others thought of me.

Oh, but nothing would be able to save Tom if he dared to follow me again. I was so over him and the drama and chaos he always seemed to bring. Yeah, not like he would ever show his face again. That was one ship which had set sail and wasn't ever going to return. Yet, somehow, he had a way of creating chaos for me from the other side of the world. And now I'd almost let him bring me down with him… again.

My phone dinged. The text read, "Mom, you there? It ok?"

A warmth filled me, spreading outward. Then the sensation finished by wrapping me from head to toe like a giant hug. My darling son, Paul, had answered. For the first time in over a year, a tiny little sliver of hope dangling before me.

Yes, he also happened to be my biggest critic. Or at least, I believed that was still true. Hard to say when we hadn't spoken in so long. In so many ways, he'd been correct in his accusations during our last conversation. Conversation might be too generous of a word. More like an all-out scream fest. Water under the bridge now. Nothing I could do to undo the harsh words said. Not his words, not mine. But as the parent, I should've begged for forgiveness. Or never have lost my temper in the first place.

Instead, I'd gone and thrown away everything I'd created in my life. My faith. My home. My job. My child, to a certain extent. Everything old now gone. All to start over again with this rundown shack in what appeared to be the worst part of town.

But explaining to my son what I was running from would be impossible. Or what I hoped to run to. Nevertheless, I had tried to tell him I still wanted to be in his life, no matter what had happened between us. But he needed to learn to stand on his own two feet without me being his constant safety net. After all, at about his age, I'd learned to be my own person.

Not true. I'm still trying to figure that one out. And I'm almost forty, for goodness' sake.

It surprised me he'd bothered to send any kind of message at all. When I'd said my peace, the gnawing in my gut assured me it would be the last I'd ever hear from him. Especially after all his allegations of how I'd been lying all those years.

Oh, I remember that discussion well, and not because it'd happened less than two years ago. Mainly because of how sideways everything went.

***

"Honey, we need to talk." I glanced over at Paul, our dinner half-finished. Him twirling his spaghetti. I'd made his favorite meal to make this night easier. Like anything could.

He switched his gaze to me. "About what?"

"I'm getting a divorce." I put my fork down on my plate. Gripping the table, my fingernails bit into the soft wood.

"You're already divorced. Dad said so." He slapped the table.

I grimaced. Yeah, this wasn't going to be a cakewalk. "No, he was mistaken on that." I gulped, trying to keep what little of my dinner I'd eaten down. "But I know how mature you are. So, I thought I'd let you decide if you wanted to live with me or go live with your father for a while." I reached over to take his hand.

He snatched it away before I could come close. My whole body recoiled at his reaction and the look of horror on his face.

"Well, duh. Dad." He threw his fork across the room. The ping of the metal reminded me of something, but it slipped away. A memory lost in time. "You kidnapped me when I was a baby! I can't believe you got away with it!"

Whoa! I hadn't seen that whopper of a lie coming. And Paul had made his pick way too fast, like he'd been waiting to be asked. What exactly had the two of them been discussing online? "I did no such thing." Bile began to rise in my throat. All I'd done was protect Paul from danger. No way to explain that now. "I'd like for you to think about this. It's a really important decision. Give me your answer tomorrow, okay?" *Why had I thought this was a good idea? To let a child make such a monumental choice?*

"Then why did we never have a house until now? Why didn't anyone ever know where we lived for like forever? And why did you never tell me anything nice about my father?" He crossed his arms over his chest in defiance, his little eyes throwing darts my way. "You're nothing but a giant liar!"

None of those things were quite the truth. We'd had a house for a while, and I'd kept my parents in the loop about the general vicinity we were in most of the time. But, yes, I'd never said anything about his missing-in-action father. Nothing good, nothing bad, nothing period. Honestly, I didn't have a clue what to say and, thus, I'd remained silent.

Okay, so this is one of those sins of omission I'm rather famous for. I should've said something to him sometime over the last ten years. But there wasn't any way to go back in time and fix this particular mistake. No more than I had a chance to repair all the others I've ever made. And I guess, in the end, this is why Paul made his choice, and he didn't pick me. He needed to learn about the other half that had helped create him.

"I don't believe I ever lied to you." I drummed my fingers on the table, rolling my eyes, trying in vain to think of a way to get this conversation back on track.

"Then why wouldn't you let Dad see me?" His fingers wiggled as he scratched at his arms.

It seemed to me he was laying a trap, but how would a child know to do this? "When?" I looked down at my plate. Red sauce was smeared across it and starting to dry. Looked like a painting Tom would do.

"My whole life! Boy, are you stupid, Mom!" He started to stand, wobbled a bit, and plunked back down.

"That's an inappropriate thing to call someone, and you know it." Yup, deflection is my friend.

"Dad said you'd deny everything! He said he was going to fight you in court and win!" A smirk bloomed on my son's face. "You're toast!"

I scrunched my face up, flicking my fingernails together. Trying to figure out what to say. Honesty I didn't feel was my best move here, because the more I said the deeper I'd end up in a hole. My child had already made his mind up long before this conversation. All based on some secret conversations with a father he'd never met in person. However, online, you can be anyone, say anything and nothing is real.

"You hated him from the moment you got married! You wouldn't let him live with you! You wouldn't support him! You yelled at him all of the time! You even tried to get him arrested more than once! He ended up going into hiding because he was so scared of what you would do! Yeah, you hate me just as much as Dad! Well, news flash, I hate you too!" His fist pounded on the table with each point. He was on a roll.

I bit my lip, tasting blood. No more. I wasn't going to sit here and be screamed at by a child. "There's no need for dramatics and accusations here. And I'm not going to respond to any of this nonsense. If you're set on living with your father, then I won't stop you. But if you do, you can't come back here. You made your bed, and you have to lie in it! You understand me?!" I tilted my head toward him, squinting my eyes. Hoping against hope he would change his mind. Despite my anger, every inch of me already ached, knowing he wasn't about to do any such thing.

"Perfect. How soon can I move out?" He jumped up, grabbing his phone from the basket on the wall.

Yeah, my one hard and fast rule had always been no phones at the table. Good gravy! I so wish I'd made the rule of no social media instead.

After the fight, we spent the next several days in awkward silence. Paul never said another word to me. Didn't matter what I said or did, he wouldn't give me a nod of his head or a look my way. And you wouldn't believe how quick Tom accepted the fact his son wanted to live with him. In less than a week, I made the drive to a town only a few hours away. Dropping my son off with strangers.

Don't even get me started on how wrong everything was. Or how Tom lived so close but never tried once to make contact with Paul until a few months ago. Tom was but a stone's throw away from my parents and had been for goodness knows how many years.

In the few days before the move, I tried to pack a few things for Paul. But he'd pushed me out of his room each time I'd dared to enter. In the end, we'd left with only two suitcases. All my son wanted from his life with me was to run away as fast as possible. Upon our arrival, my heart sank. The place wasn't a house. Nothing more than a rundown apartment building with junk lying around everywhere. Tom didn't bother to come out to greet us. He stood in the doorframe glaring at us.

Paul pulled one suitcase out of the trunk, I grabbed the other, and I started to go up the walk. Paul shoved me hard with his elbow as he yanked the handle out of my hand. Turning his back on me, he marched toward his father. Never looking back, no words of goodbye. My silent tears flowed as the person who was my heart entered the apartment. The door closed with a slam, swallowing my son and his father. With my heart in my throat, I wanted to scream 'no' until I became hoarse.

Everything I'd done to protect my child had been for nothing. Everything I'd done to help my husband had led to this moment. And all of it had been wrong.

***

As I now stood on the threshold of a new chapter, I sensed that, if I kept looking back, all I'd see would be mistakes. Oh, so many blunders and errors were made. One of the joys of getting older I guess was being able to look back at a long life of nothing but regrets. Would'ves, could'ves, should'ves, and what-ifs. Nothing more.

"Found my own little slice of heaven," I typed in a rapid reply to Paul. I hit send before allowing myself a second to give in to the temptation to add more. I'd tackle the rest of our family complications another day. Then I started to walk up the stairs to my new life, a definite spring in my feet at the idea my son might change his mind.

Chapter 5

Shaking my head again to try and remove the cobwebs, I grasped the doorknob as firmly as possible. With my fingers trembling like leaves during a strong windstorm, I had a hard time getting the key in the lock. With a loud tick, the key tapped against the metal and then slipped into the slot and turned as if by magic.

As I started to pry open the door of my new home, the door got rather stuck. I hit at it with most of my body, giving it a good shove with my shoulder. With an echoing pop, a large crack appeared, then a bat whipped by my head and out into the late afternoon shadows. Startled, I almost fell and grabbed the porch railing beside me for support. The wooden piece crumbled to nothing in my clenched fist.

Laughing at both my fright and the sawdust left in my grip, I brushed the dust off onto my jeans. Staring at the tree in front of the house for a moment, I hoped to spy my vacated visitor. After a moment, my neck spasmed and I gave up. At least the bat wasn't inside anymore.

Turning back to the entrance, I scanned the opening for evidence of more intruders. Pulling a flashlight out of a pocket in my backpack, I waved it up and down into the gloom of the front hall for a second or two. Nothing else emerged from within, though more than a few eyeballs peered back at me from the dark recess. Every inch of me developed goosebumps at the thought of who or what lurked behind those eyes. My stomach twisted at the thought of the creatures that might be waiting for me inside.

"Miss, why ya here?" a faint, unsure voice called to me. Jumping, my heart fluttered, though the sound came from behind, not in front of me. Putting my hand to my chest to ensure I was still among the living, I exhaled with a massive sigh of relief.

Spinning around, I spotted a young man on the crumbling sidewalk. He leaned on an old bike, one tire flat the blue of the frame so faded it was almost indiscernible. The boy had skin the color of burned wood. His black hair curly and sticking up every which way. His green shorts and yellow shirt were grimy and worn and several sizes too large. I estimated his age around fourteen or fifteen. I wasn't sure why he wasn't in school. Short day perhaps? Or did school here always get out before three in the afternoon? Guess it wasn't my affair.

"I live here," giving him a flash of a smile. I started to go bit by bit down the steps toward him, half afraid the wood beneath my feet would cave in as the railing had.

"Oh no ya don't, lady. Dat place be haunted. No one live in it in like forever!" His whole body shivered; his eyes bigger than serving platters. "Ya crazy?" One hand went up to his mouth while the other struggled to keep his bike standing.

I stopped midway down the stairs. Well, it wasn't the first time I'd lived someplace people claimed was haunted. Most people believed the first house I'd ever owned to be haunted as well, maybe because it had burned to the ground years ago. Not like I ever believed the crying in the night I heard so often was anything more than the wind. Yet no one ever explained how the fire had started. Or how it'd burned so hot and quick. But I had a pretty good idea and ghosts had nothing to do with it. My body gave a fast little shiver at the thought as I tried to stuff that memory back into the vault.

"Why do you think it's haunted?" I sat down on the steps, wanting to have a pleasant chat rather than this weird conversation. But my reward turned out to be a nail sticking me in a very uncomfortable place. I shifted a little and got pinched by a loose board for my efforts. Ugh.

"Miss Samuel's brother got murdered here." The words were spoken with an easy calm, as if a violent death was no big deal.

Odd. Ghosts he feared, but criminals he didn't? Oh my, how many gangsters and thieves lived around here? Must be why the cab driver fled quicker than a flash of lightning.

He set his bike down in the tall grass. It became invisible in a second as the slim stalks swayed on the breeze. He took a hesitant hop toward me. "Why ya here?" he said, repeating his question from earlier.

Just my luck. I bought a house where a murder had taken place. Must be why I got the place for a song – and the fact it was ready to crumble into nothing. "Well, I'm here because..." I stopped, cocked my head a tiny bit to glance at my new friend. "First, tell me your name."

"Hank." He came over to plop next to me on the well-worn steps. He mopped at the sweat dripping from his brow with a rag he'd pulled from his back pocket. He shook his sweaty shirt a little in addition. Don't think it did much in the long run.

"Well, Hank, my name's Amy." I took his large hand in mine, ignoring the clamminess. "Nice to meet you. Are we neighbors?" I took a quick sweeping peek down the street, trying in vain to pick out a house which showed signs of life. Most were in worse shape than mine. Not a car in sight anywhere. Nor any humans. A lone dog wandered up the road, his tongue hanging low because of the heat. Seems I'd managed to end up in a ghost town in the middle of a city.

His head dipped in a small nod in agreement. Reaching deep into my backpack, I hauled out my bag of snacks I'd packed for my bus ride. I hadn't touched them much on the trip, so I had lots of things to pick from. Then I yanked out a couple of juice boxes.

Placing the goodies between us, I said, "I can tell you my story, but I don't think I'll be able to finish in one day or a week for that matter, and I want to hear more about this house. Can you come back again?"

Don't ask why my mood led me to make this child my confessor. Could've been nothing more than him being here with me at a moment of weakness. Or the fact he looked about the same age as my son. The one person I should've told the truth to was my son, not some strange child. Still, if my mind started dwelling on the rift between my child and me, I'd end up thinking about things I didn't wish to dwell on.

No, it's simple. The heat made me want to do nothing more than take a time out, have something almost cool to drink, and watch the world go by. Tugging my hair off the nape of my neck for a moment, I wished for a fan. The air felt so oppressive a body could drown on land around here.

But then again, if I told Hank my truth, maybe I'd finally find the courage to tell Paul. He deserved to hear what was real and what wasn't. Yeah, with how things stood at the moment, this was going to be so much harder to do. Yet, Paul might be learning the hard way some of the things I needed to tell him.

"Yup, lady, ya crazy 'nuf to be here. I crazy 'nuf to come. Get betta snacks next time!" He grabbed a bag of chips and began to eat as if he hadn't had anything for days. Teenagers are the same no matter where you go. "Funyuns betta…" he mumbled with his mouth full.

My heart cried out for my son, for those times like these when he and I had relaxed and done nothing much. I looked down at my hands. I had to stop thinking about that fight we'd had. That argument would destroy me if I didn't. I never should've given an ultimatum.

Turning my mind to the present, I examined Hank as he munched on his treat. Deciding if, in fact, I should tell him anything and if so, where to begin. Breathing in deep, I figured I'd just keep going where I'd left off in my head earlier. The early days with Tom.

"Well, my story started with my odd husband. Before that, it wasn't very interesting. But, you see, my husband abandoned me the morning after our wedding ceremony, and I moved without telling him since he wasn't available to say anything to. Oh, and this happened when I wasn't much older than you." My hand tapped on my leg as I started to remember my college days.

Chapter 6

I'm not exactly sure when in my freshman year that Tom, my wayward husband, dared to show back up. Time has a way of blurring memory and softening the harshest of pains. But late one night, I returned to my tiny apartment after a grueling day of work, school, work, studying, and perhaps a bite to eat in between. Only to fall into a deep sleep as soon as I found a moment to hit my pillow. A normal nose-to-the-grindstone existence.

Such a lovely bright sunny day. Green grass as far as the eye could see. Cute red and white checked blanket. Wicker basket overflowing with fresh, homemade goodies to eat. Faint breeze blowing my hair out of my eyes. I'm on a picnic lunch with the man of my dreams.

Wait! Why is his face blank? There are no eyes, nose, or mouth! Why is the sun beginning to fade? What is that pounding? Thud, thud, thud, over and over again. I woke with the sharp realization that everything had been a dream. Still safe in my bed, I found my attempt at sleeping for a few precious hours a total failure. But the knocking was all too real.

Groaning, I rolled over to squint at the clock. However, my bed was so tiny I ended up in a heap on the floor twisted up in my blankets. Wondering who dared to bang on my door in the middle of the night, I rubbed my right elbow which now throbbed. I got a better view of the clock. Crud, a little after two AM. I hoped if I ignored the idiot, they would go away. So, I laid as still as a mouse on the floor while looking up at the clock. One minute passed and the thumps continued. Two minutes passed, a heartbeat more. Rather obvious that I must do something before the neighbors started screaming.

Mrs. Diaz in particular – she had a new baby and didn't like it when people made noise during the day. An itty bitty, little noise, like me turning the key in my door and bumping my shopping bags against the frame as I did so was way too loud. You wouldn't believe how much she yelled at me over that. You could've heard her a few blocks away. Her Spanish rang out for miles upon miles.

Pulling my fuzzy bathrobe over the oversized, long-sleeved t-shirt I wore as a nightgown, I shivered. Throwing my bedding in a heap in the middle of the bed to keep it a bit warmer for later, I growled. All of me regretted getting out from under my six blankets and two comforters. No longer between my flannel sheets, I moaned as the cold air hit me. Yes, I never turned on the heat unless it got below forty degrees outside.

Back then, I had to think hard about what to set the thermostat to – 50 or 55 degrees. Who has the money for the necessities in life? I sure never did in those days of struggling for a grain of rice. And I was only in the beginning stage of my journey of learning that what doesn't kill you only makes you stronger. Plus gives you lots of ammunition. Unfortunately for me, I never used those bullets for anything important.

I padded through my darkened apartment, the cracked laminate floor ice under my bare feet. The cold doing a slow crawl up my ankles to my calves. Yes, a semi-awake state appeared to be the best I could do at that point. But no way turning on a light would be better. That might force me to be all the way awake making this whole nightmare real.

Looking out the peephole, I saw nothing but darkness. The stupid landlord still hadn't fixed the light on the landing. Since the day I'd moved in, that burned-out bulb had remained up there. When I tried to replace the light myself, I found out the blockhead of a landlord had locked the thing covering the bulb.

But since the bangs on the door were still a steady drumbeat, I had to resolve the problem at hand. Light or no light.

"Who's there?" I called out through my paper-thin hollow-core door. To be honest, I hadn't a clue how the person's fist hadn't punched right into my apartment. The door wasn't ever meant to be anything more than a closet door. I didn't comprehend at all why it had a lock on it. There was no reason. One hard push and you'd be inside. Yes, I lived in a super safe place for a semi-single girl. But the apartment rented out cheap and low rent was my best friend.

"Honey, I'm home!" A booming, heavy male voice came back in reply.

Okay, not helpful but at least the thumping noise had stopped. Still, Mrs. Diaz would spit kittens in the morning. However, since I didn't understand half of what she said most of the time, I tended to take what she said with a grain of salt. So, pretending she had just shared a great cookie recipe in the most animated way imaginable was always possible. And preferable to the alternative.

"And you are?" Half leaning on the wall next to the door, I wanted nothing more than to go back to my blissful state of unconsciousness in my warm bed. As I didn't come by enough sleep on a normal day, this interruption wasn't helpful.

"Oh, Amy, I'm Tom. We got married yesterday, remember? How could you forget me so soon? You said you loved me. You promised we'd be together forever..." He sounded close to tears, his voice catching on every other word.

What?! This had to be some kind of joke, right? Some friends of mine were playing some horrible unfunny prank on me! Because if Tom, my supposed husband, had reappeared, something was very wrong. Our wedding was more than six months ago, not yesterday! And I didn't remember telling anyone about my sort of marriage since moving here. So, how had my Houdini of a husband arrived on my doorstep? Gulping down the lump in my throat, I almost didn't want to know the answer to this.

Cracking open the door as much as the safety chain would allow, I tried to get a better gauge of the person at my door. In the darkness, it was impossible to tell who the person might be. A dim light illuminated his face for a few moments and a spark of recognition shot through me. He looked so different now. Long scruffy beard and mustache, long dirty, matted hair, and sunken cheeks. Nowhere close to the man I'd married. Back then, his hair had been trimmed short with no facial hair at all. And he'd been just about spotless. Seemed Tom was a man of a thousand faces. Oh, yeah, that's right, the guys had cleaned him up before the wedding. I guess he didn't have anyone to rely on now.

"See, here's us yesterday." His voice rose an octave or two too high. It hurt my ears.

He turned a hand toward me that held a picture of us. His other hand angled a flashlight beam onto the photo. A snap from our reception. I wore my dress, looking bored, but he looked almost normal in his suit, not like the homeless person now standing before me. But that might as well have been a lifetime ago, so much had happened in such a short period of time. I had no idea how he had gotten the picture; I didn't have one. Not like I wanted one.

"Why didn't you stay at our house? I planned everything. Our life was going to be so perfect." He sounded like a little boy who had lost his favorite toy and didn't have a clue how to find it.

"That was months ago. I had almost no money, a bad job, and was unsure where you were. How'd you find me? And why are you here now?" I didn't give him an inch; my stare wasn't a welcoming one. You know the famous 'if looks could kill' one. Maybe if he had shown up in the daytime, maybe if he looked better, maybe if it had been less time....

"Oh, sorry about that. Anywho, I'm here because I couldn't find you at our home. That made me so sad, but everyone said you were here." He laughed in this weird, creepy way that made my skin crawl. You know, like bugs walking all over you. It took most of my effort to not throw up.

Pulling my robe tighter, I tried to think of a way out of this situation. Stupid me for writing my mother once I'd rented the apartment. Yup, she'd blabbed to the whole town where I'd gone to. And I could only imagine the gossip going around now that he'd turned up in my tiny hometown again. Asking where in the heck I'd disappeared to after I'd lied and said he'd moved here first. My plan for getting out of the mess had failed. But he was my husband for better or for worse. These words had come from my lips, that pledge had been made. Thus, I must do something besides calling the police and reporting an intruder.

With a sigh loud enough to shake the pathetic door I said, "Can you go somewhere else tonight? We can talk tomorrow. It's so late, and I'm really tired after a long day."

"No, sorry, babe, no can do. My mom told me I can't live in the basement anymore now that I've gone and got married. She made me give her the key to the house before the wedding." Tears were in his voice as he said this. His momma had broken his heart. "But I'm all yours. Ain't it wonderful? My first apartment! Super cool!" Now he started jumping up and down, clapping his hands like a kid who'd gotten the toy he'd asked for from Santa.

The swing of his emotions was beyond dizzying. In the space of a few seconds, he'd gone from depressed to manic. I'd never met anyone else able to do that. Was that a good thing? Was that in any way normal? *Oh my goodness, Amy, of course this isn't normal! Nothing about his guy is typical or ordinary in any way, shape, or form!*

In my rush to the altar in less than a week, why didn't I bother to ask this guy any questions? Questions like, did he have a real job that pays him money, not banana chips? Did he receive his driver's license from a cereal box rather than the driver's license place? Was his mother married to his uncle? How close to being committed to the funny farm was he? I knew nothing about this man. Was I one hundred percent sure what his real name was? Yikes, this lack of knowledge slapped me in the face after only a few hours of marriage.

This led me to another problem. How much had my father known? Because his words before the wedding now came back to haunt me. "Even in the Bible, sometimes marriages weren't always perfect but were part of God's plan." By now, I was convinced he'd heard about that wild night of Tom's before the wedding. Not like I'd asked my father about it specifically. But was my father aware of more issues than that? He never once appeared fazed by the fact that Tom went missing after the ceremony.

Gladness overwhelmed me that the room remained dark. Tom couldn't see my face. I felt how enormous my scowl was. How hard I scrunched up my nose. How tight my eyes pulled in. My whole face hurt as I clenched and unclench my teeth. I never wore this expression. No, I'm a Pollyanna on any other given day. Nothing got me down. My smile always remains planted on. Until now.

Hate. Hate filled me. I was sure this feeling didn't become me. Bad enough I had this sensation of loathing. No way did I want anyone else to see it. How was it possible I despised the man I had married? What had I turned into? How could I undo this – my hate and my marriage?

No, very deep breath here. In, out, in, out. Puffing out my cheeks, I worked my jaw around to release some of my pent-up tension.

Marriage is sacred. Marriage is love. God is love. His children must love.

Another huge deep breath now, all the way down to my toes. I repeated these words to myself several times like a mantra. I must love everyone, including my enemy. How did I end up marrying an enemy? Oh, gracious me, what a catastrophe. It was like I'd woken up and found myself on the Titanic.

"Ah, come on, sweetheart. Let me sleep with you. We're married and we haven't even made it official yet!" He pushed his fingers through the crack, attempting to reach out and touch me. Wiggling those fingers like worms, he got closer and closer to my arm.

Jumping back in disgust, I knocked over the shoe stand with a clatter. With my skin on fire, I patted and rubbed myself down, trying to gain some control over the feelings creeping over me. Biting my lip, I replied, "You can't. I only have a twin bed."

Yup, true statement. I hadn't furnished the rental house in my hometown. Thus, I'd ended up sleeping on a blowup mattress from my camping gear the whole time. And when I moved to this college town, I'd gotten a small bed, dresser, loveseat-sized couch, bookshelf, end table, and not much more. And almost all of it nothing more than used junk from a thrift store.

"Sleep in your truck. I don't care," I managed to huff out. Well, I'd lied, another thing I didn't do on a typical day before my marriage. I used to be so honest that most people said it was painful to listen to. Yeah, by now, you know me – I've been half lying about my marriage from the get-go. No one in this town was aware of my marital state, and I do mean, no one. Uhm, at least not as far as I was privy to. But in this case, I did care what Tom did, an awful lot. I needed him to remove himself from my life. He needed to obtain the annulment, which I couldn't bring myself to go to the courthouse and acquire. For the simple reason that I didn't want to disappoint my father. My father had picked this man for whatever reason and told me I had to be a woman of my word. No way was I going back on that. If Tom broke our sacred vows, I'd be free to stick with my happy, carefree, and pretend single life that I'd carved out for myself.

"Fine, whatever. Have to say, babe, you're a bit of a downer." His fingernails scratched against the door.

Was he sulking? If he was, chalk up another mood swing. I'd been sticking with displeased since I came to the door, so why was he all over the map? Upset, sad, happy, disappointed, you name it. He'd experienced emotions I'd didn't think existed. The middle of the night wasn't the proper time to deal with mood swings. As if there was a perfect time for having a conversation like that.

As firm as I could, I pushed the door closed and locked it up tight. Hoping no fingers got smushed in the process. My feet padded back across the freezing floor to my room, and I went back to snuggling in my bed. Of course, I did slide the cheap, fiberboard dresser in front of my door before flopping onto my mattress still with my robe on. Just in case he decided to push through the cheap front door. Or he didn't believe me about how small my bed is – I wasn't taking any chances. The dresser wouldn't have stopped a charging cat. Even filled with my clothes, it only weighed something like thirty pounds. But the symbolism of it made me feel a teensy bit better.

The tangy, acidic odor of smoke greeted me in the morning. I rolled over to squint at my old-fashioned windup alarm clock. Ick. Just a few minutes before it would go off anyway. Ugh. Today I so wanted to sleep in. No such luck there. Work, school, and whatever caused the smell awaited me. Since none of the smoke detectors blared, the response from my brain was rather sluggish. Nor did it register the fact a threat to my life may be in the works.

In a sleep-deprived daze, I dressed in a rush like my house might be on fire. *Please let last night be some crazy dream. Please let Tom not be in my life again. Please let me not be smelling smoke right now.* I kept saying all of that to myself under my breath as I did my best to throw some clothes on.

Sliding the dresser away from the door frame, I gritted my teeth so hard, in fact, I bit my tongue. The taste of blood sour in my mouth as I hesitated for a moment before my door. As I debated about jumping out the window instead, I ticked my fingers on the wall. But two stories were a long way to fall down.

Opening the door a crack, I peeked through and saw nothing amiss in the tiny hall. The bathroom looked safe and untouched as I crept by on my tiptoes. I ignored the darkened cave of the kitchen area because a beacon pulled me forward. The front room glowed in the early morning light. Odd. I always closed the blinds before I went to bed. But now the mini-blinds were missing from the windows.

Walking the final few steps to my living room, I spotted a form huddled under a blanket on the floor near the couch. I'd have to deal with the case of the missing blinds later. But they had better be somewhere, because I wasn't giving up my security deposit without a fight. Yeah, pennies scream around me because I pinch them so hard.

But the person on the floor was an even bigger problem. My thinking the night before proved to be correct, my lock was pointless. A toddler could've opened my front door without me even knowing it. Thus, here I stood, looking down at Tom. The man I'd had the misfortune of marrying had broken into my house. I did a quick scan of the room, looking for something to defend myself with. I grabbed the lamp off the side table. Feeling more than a bit foolish, I put it back down. The stupid thing was only one of those tiny candle-shaped ones that are about three inches long. Plus, it was made from cheap plastic. I'd hurt myself more than I'd damage anyone or anything else.

Smoke wafted up from inside one of my good coffee cups sitting on the floor next to the still figure. And by good, I mean one of the few items in my home that was purchased new. A housewarming gift from my mother. She'd sent off me to school with them. But the little bit of smoke didn't give the impression it was enough of an inferno to make the whole place have the ode de smoke aroma. Perhaps he'd been smoking for a while and the fumes were residual.

Wonderful. My dishes had become ashtrays. Not to mention the no smoking policy my apartment had. Think hard now. Must be some way of getting this odor out of here before the landlord found out, and I lost my deposit for breaking his rules. My mind came up with nothing but a complete blank. Potpourri didn't seem like it'd be strong enough to remove the stench. How did I not have any idea Tom smoked? Guess that was another one of those questions I should've asked. Do you smoke or drink? Well, in my mind, I checked off both those boxes. Oh, my heavens, kill me now.

Since the still figure hadn't moved, I decided to disregard the problems in the living room for a moment. I turned to go into the one space I'd yet to examine. Entering the tiny u-shaped galley kitchen area, I flipped on the light. The mess before me took my breath away and left my stomach churning in anger. My stove now caked with bits of burnt bread and eggs stuck on every surface. Raw egg dripped down the front of the stove and cabinets onto the floor. Milk splashed from the fridge to the stove. Soggy cornflakes had exploded onto every surface of the kitchen, including the walls. Every dish I owned looked like they were on the counter or in the sink, all covered in something disgusting. Then, something wet dribbled onto my face, running in a long smear. Looking up at my pot rack hanging on the wall, I spotted my pots had remained undisturbed. So, if Tom had tried to cook something, he was insane enough to do it without a pan.

Or else the only thing he had washed and returned turned out to be a pan.

Brushing my hand against the wet spot on my cheek, I realized it was mustard. Glancing up again, I got a better glimpse at my ceiling. Condiments – at least I hoped that's what the paint used on the mural up there was. Bright yellow, red, orange, and green spots were everywhere. Who knows what it was supposed to depict. Seemed like one of those crazy modern art pieces. You know the kind that, in theory, should be a woman cradling a child. In reality, they looked like a monkey had thrown paint at a board for ten minutes and called it a day. With any luck, my landlord would love it because it would be a bear to clean off if he didn't. How had Tom done this much damage to such a small space in only a few hours? Husband or no, he couldn't stay another minute. It'd been a huge error in judgment on my part to have spoken to him for even a second. Or for not calling the cops on him.

Marching into the living room, I noticed the lump on the floor hadn't moved an inch. "Tom! How dare you break in here! What were you thinking? Trashing my apartment like this! Get up right this instant and get out of my apartment!"

The temptation to kick at the huge bump filled me. But I resisted with every ounce of strength in my small frame. My hands were clenched at my sides, punching my thighs. A verse came to me right then: 'Beloved, let us love one another, for love is from God; and everyone who loves is born of God and knows God.' But right now, love was the farthest thing from what I wanted to do. I started to massage the soft fabric of my skirt, willing myself to be calm. But my whole body got hit with lightning over and over again. The jolts made me want to break something. Or someone.

As he stood up, the blanket slid off to reveal he wasn't wearing any clothes. And by that, I mean nada, no socks, nothing.

"Okay, don't be such a downer, babe. Let me finish my joint first." He wasn't looking at me, he stared up at the wall behind me instead. As far as he was concerned, I wasn't important at all in this situation. Or he was so high, focusing was impossible.

"Where are your clothes?! Wrap yourself back up in the blanket for goodness' sake." I turned so he became a little blurry in the corner of my eye. I felt my blush spreading from my toes to my hair. This wasn't how I wanted to see a naked man for the first time. "And stop smoking! Don't you think you've done enough damage?!"

"Slow your roll, hon. I threw my clothes out the door. Fabric is sooo confining, don't you know. Our skin was made to breathe. So, I try to be free as much as possible." He jiggled his lower body a bit. "You should try it, sweetie."

My blush deepened from a dull pink to crimson. He grabbed what I now understood to be a joint from the cup and took a hit before bending over to pick up the throw. The cloth cascaded in a soft drape as he only held it up in front of him enough to conceal most of his manly bits. This left his whole backside exposed. For someone who didn't want to wear clothes, he was rather white. Not a hint of a farmer's tan, no color at all. Don't ask me why I looked. It was wrong of me to do so, I was sure. My purity had leapt out the window at this point. I wouldn't be able to claim nothing had happened in this marriage any longer. No way to unsee what I stood there gawking at.

"I'll go find my pants if I must." He started for the door.

"NO! My neighbors will see you! Besides, I doubt your things will be anywhere near here. Mr. Diaz works rather early in the morning and picks up all the trash around as he walks to his truck." I guess I could thank my lucky stars he'd broken into my home still wearing clothing.

Nevertheless, beyond that, I had some major issues. There went my reputation. What will people think with men's clothing hanging from my balcony railing for my next-door neighbor to find? Assuming his things had landed in that general vicinity. At least my now bare windows faced nothing but the empty lot next door. Oh, and the parking area in front since my apartment is in the corner. Plus, I'm on the second floor, that would help ward against any would-be peeping toms.

Thus, I had a sliver of hope that no one I knew would or could see him standing in his birthday suit in my living room. Or find out he was smoking dope. I rolled my eyes at that thought.

Taking a huge gulp of air to calm my nerves, curiosity got the better of me. "What happened in the kitchen? And why didn't the smoke detectors go off?" I spun a tiny amount because I found myself ogling at things I'd rather not be looking at. Sure, I married the man, but it felt borderline criminal to be doing what we were doing. Yet I had a hard time pulling my eyes away. My head did a slow crawl from my chin on my chest to pointing at the ceiling. My eyes spun in their attempt to get a glimpse of anything or anywhere but at him. His scrawny hairless, sunk in chest. His chicken arms and legs. And more. Ugh, the sight repulsed me. However, I still glanced his way every other second.

"Got the munchies; made a snack. Your stove didn't work like my mom's and the eggs wouldn't stay on the burner. The fork's way too small so the toast fell off. The bowls you've got make my fingers tingle in a weird way and I kept dropping them. So, yeah, um, the cereal didn't work either. Finally gave up and just painted for a while. Had to relax, you know, babe. Oh, and, well, I smashed all your detectors and threw them out the door with my clothes. Oh, and the blinds. No need to let the government spies know I'm here and what I'm doing. Bugs are everywhere."

He rolled his head in a slow rotation and took another hit from the joint. He didn't return it to the cup this time. Instead, it dangled from his long fingers with such a light touch it appeared to be floating in the air. Afraid it might fall to the floor, I almost asked him if he wanted me to take it from him. But no way in heck did I want to touch a marijuana joint.

"Okay, I'm sure they know I'm here, but they don't need to listen to our conversations." He sighed. "Privacy is king." He gave me an amused, wicked smile, his eyebrows going up and down faster and faster.

Great, a conspiracy theory nut job on top of everything else. This wasn't something I needed and or wanted to deal with. I didn't have any training in psych yet. If I remembered the handout, it was taught around junior year. I was only a freshman. Tom and his whacked-out theories were going to have to wait for another day. Or better still, find someone else to feed those lines to.

"What are you talking about?" Hippies? Nudists? Spies? How much dope did this guy use? "And I told you to put that cigarette out! I'm going to get kicked out of here if my landlord ever finds out anyone was smoking in here." My gaze snapped up to his face. Enough of this! He needed to leave my house. Now. I didn't need or want this drama in my life.

He laughed, his eyes twinkling, his facial hair shuddering with the effort. "Chill. It's only a little joint. You gotta take a hit and relax, sweetheart. Mellow out. You're so tense, girl." He hummed a tune, twirling in an odd dance. I stared at this behavior for a moment, unsure what I should do. Before I could frame any type of response, he stopped dead.

"You were drunk at our wedding!" This accusation flung out in an attempt to get him to see his many wrongs. Not like he cared, I'm sure, but I was going to have my say. "You left me without saying anything about where you were going. I don't even know where you work."

"No biggie. You gotta go with the flow, do what feels good, do what you wanna do, go where you wanna go. My way of living is so easy…." His feet shuffled on the floor for a moment before he collapsed in a heap.

"No, you don't get off that easy! Stand up and face me like a man! I waited months for you. I put up with all of these crazy rumors because of you, and now you're trying to destroy everything I've worked so hard for!" I snatched the joint out of his hand. Less because I wanted to put it out, more because it now rested on the floor. I was afraid the whole apartment would burn down. Rushing back into the kitchen, I turned the water on and put the vile thing under the flow. Finished off by trying to stuff it down the drain. Without warning, I sensed hot breath on my neck.

He grasped my wrist tight. "No, that's my last one!" He pulled what little was left of the soggy mess out of the sink. Giant tears streamed down his face as he sank to the floor, clutching his hand into a fist. He rocked back and forth, moaning.

And I was done with the drama of the morning. The pain of a migraine coming on started to hit me, so I turned and stormed out the front door with as much haste as possible. In a neat pile beside my welcome mat were Tom's clothes, now folded. Picking them up, I tossed them into my apartment before slamming the door shut.

Chapter 7

"Lady, ya's crazy. Ya making up tales." Hank laughed deep from his belly as he leaned back on the steps, propped on his elbows. He'd cut into my story, thoughts, and memories, and I wasn't sure I welcomed the intrusion.

"Scout's honor, I'm speaking the truth here." I held up three fingers as proof. My face grim. I didn't want to argue or justify myself to a stranger I'd met such a short time ago. "It's late now; enough talk for today. I haven't stepped inside yet. You run off home and have some dinner. These snacks aren't a real meal. We'll talk more another day, okay?" I pushed him in the small of his damp back to encourage him to jump up and head home. Wishing for all the world I'd kept my gigantic trap shut and said nothing.

Truth is truth, whether people agree with it or not. I wasn't about to sugarcoat my story because someone didn't believe it or like it. But this wasn't a new problem; I've faced this issue before. And it was why I'd become famous for that sin of omission. I often didn't speak up when I should've. Don't think it would've made much of a difference if I had; the rumors would've still been flying no matter what.

"Yup. I gotta bounce." He wiggled off the stairs and sauntered over to his bike. Pulling it up from the weeds, he plopped it onto the sidewalk with a whack. I gazed at him as he hopped on and wobbled down the street. Why he didn't walk the bike rather than try to ride the thing with a flat, I couldn't figure out. Guess it's a boy thing, trying to be all macho for no real reason. My son had been the same way. Hank turned the corner, gone without another word.

My heart lurched at the thought of returning to my task of entering my new home. All of those eyeballs inside had dampened my enthusiasm a bit. Didn't feel like this could be an instant home for me after all. But I didn't have another option here; I'd slammed shut all the other doors in my life. Once inside, the assault on my nose from the dank odor of musky animal, mold, damp, and rot hit me like a gut punch. Years of neglect hadn't been kind to the place, not one little bit. The stench strong enough to make my eyes water and my stomach do more than a few flip flops.

But a pleasant surprise awaited me. I couldn't see the sky above me through the roof. Also, I spotted no cracks in the exterior walls as I swiveled my head around. Still, it'd be best to have the shell inspected by a pro at some point. But as I had feared, all the walls were stripped to bare studs. No wiring, no plumbing, no sheetrock, no toilet, no sink, and no shower. The floors were the rough subfloors only.

As the faint glow from my flashlight shown around, my eyes caught on very little but stale air. The open area allowed everything to flow through the exposed interior walls. It was possible to shine my light from the front to the back without a problem, the beam only catching on more than a few spider webs and motes of dust. A total gut job, a blank canvas to create a whole new space out of. The exact same thing as my life at the moment.

Yet, all in all, I was more prepared for the shoddy condition of the house than this point in my life where I abandoned everything. That moment I'd said, "Enough's enough," and moved here to this unknown corner of the world. Well, unknown to me at least. But that was the point.

In my giant suitcases, I had a folding broom/mop combo, an inflatable mattress, cleaning supplies, a single burner propane stove, and the propane. Plus, food, water, and other items I considered essentials.

This is why I'd taken the bus and not a plane. These items weren't allowed on flights. Heck, I doubted they allowed these on the bus either. But unlike airports, bus depots almost never check to find out what's in your luggage. And you were often the one to place your bags on the bus, not an employee. Made life easier when you were trying to uproot your whole life in a few days and take only what you could carry with you.

Yes, I could've driven to my new home. But to be honest, fear stopped me. Thus, I'd sold my little old Ford Ranger before I'd left. Silly, I know. Here I am, almost in my forties, moving all the way across the country alone, but I couldn't face the idea of driving that far by myself. When I got ready – yikes, if I ever got comfortable with the insane amount of traffic around here, I'd buy another car. The rat race wasn't for me. Never had been.

What I'd seen during the cab ride was enough to scare me off driving for the rest of my life. When you're used to rush-hour being five people and a cattle drive, driving isn't a major deal. Thus, this part of big city life wasn't for me, not with cars zipping in and around each other. Horns blaring, giving people the finger, and missing another car by an inch. Yup, I'd only had one quick trip in this town so far and I was so over the way these people drove. I'll walk everywhere, thank you very much.

Okay, this town wasn't a true big city. I'm not foolish enough to think otherwise. It wasn't like I'd moved to Atlanta or Miami or New Orleans. How many people were residents of the town I'd ended up in wasn't the deciding factor here. Nope, the important fact was I've never been here before. And it didn't hurt that the state was a thousand miles from anywhere I've ever come close to before. A place where I can tell my story or not. And it was large enough I could fade into the woodwork and not be the constant source of gossip as I had been for years. Who was I kidding? Gossip has been swirling like a fog around me most of my adult life. Nothing I ever did had been able to shake it and allow some sunshine in. Until now. I'd left those people with the wagging tongues far behind.

The next morning, I woke refreshed, my very soul lighter than it had ever been. My first night had been so pleasant and peaceful. After I chased out most of the birds, bats, squirrels, and that darned opossum, that is. Oh, and cleaned everything as best I could, inflated my bed, cooked my dinner in the backyard, and goodness only knows what other chores I'd done. All the while sweating in places I didn't think you could sweat. The insane heat that hadn't let up since the second I'd arrived in this city. I'd slept like a rock because exhaustion made me unable to move. Same way I always slept in my old life; I've always been a hard worker. Don't ever believe anyone who tells you otherwise.

Today, the determination to buy a ladder filled every inch of me. I desired to remove the plywood from the windows. The house felt like living in a damp, hot cave once I'd managed to wrestle the door closed. No easy feat getting the door to move even an inch, don't know when was the last time anyone had tried to open it. The frame and the door were no longer the same size. The reason could only be the crazy humidity.

Oh, I know I should've made my life easier and left the door open to provide some fresh air. The smell in the place had given me quite the headache by morning. But leaving it open didn't feel safe somehow, not with all the talk of murder from Hank. Leaving the windows open instead was just the ticket. And, as an added bonus, I'd be able to have a better look at the roof as well. Once some sunlight streamed inside from the windowpanes, everything would be visible. The good, the bad, and the horrendous.

As I lay stretching like a cat in bed, a knock on the door startled me out of my musings. Curling into a ball for a moment, I debated about answering or not. But the new me, the I'm-not-afraid-of-anyone me, had no options. I leapt off my mattress. Okay, I crawled. The thing lay on the bare floor after all.

Pulling on some pants and a shirt over the tank top I'd worn to bed to try to stay cool, I called out, "One minute please!" I rushed to the entrance, still tugging down my blouse.

Dragging the door open with some difficulty, I spied a tall, older handsome man on my doorstep. "Good morning. How may I help you?" I asked, polite as could be as if I expected company at my glorious mansion on this fine day. I patted down my hair, wiggling a little to free my pant legs from my perspiring calves.

"No." He handed me a card before fleeing like my house was on fire and rushed to a truck waiting on the curb. "No! No!" he exclaimed as he flapped his hands in the air, not turning around at all.

"Wait! Who are you?" I called after him, waving the card in my hand. But I was too late, he climbed in the vehicle and drove off. Nothing more, nothing less.

The card advertised a handyman service along with a name printed on it. Hmm. Did this guy drive around looking for work? No, that didn't make any sense. Nothing on the outside of this property had changed since yesterday. Somehow, he knew I was here. Shivering at the thought of someone watching my every move, I gave a hasty glance at my front door. My spine tingled with icy fingers going up and down like they were playing the piano. Nope, the whole entrance was solid wood. Not like that door from my first apartment in college. It would take more than a bit of force to push through it. Still, I mentally added deadbolts to my list of things I needed to buy today. No one would end up in my home unannounced on my watch ever again.

And for some reason, about then, I realized no mailbox stood next to the curb. With slow strides, I walked down my steps so I could see up and down the street. Only a few of the other homes had mailboxes. *Is it as simple as I put one up and hope for the best? Or should I find the nearest post office and ask what the proper thing to do is?* I shook my head at this new problem and at the sad thought that no new neighbors were around to have chats with over coffee. When I had a table, that is. For the simple reason, no one lived in this area. I'd been correct in my thoughts on this the day before. So where had Hank come from exactly?

Turning back around, I spotted a ladder propped against the side of my house. Oh my, a magic hardware fairy had left me a gift. As I approached it with the same care I would a coiled snake, I saw no note or any hint on how the thing had managed to arrive. Underneath the ladder sat a toolbox. Again, there was nothing to say who the owner might be or who'd left it. Must be from my odd caller, one John Collins, according to the card.

I gnawed on my lower lip for a moment, pondering what to do about the tools. Do I use them or not? Well, if I did, it would save me a headache for a bit and a trip to the store for supplies. Had the guy intended to do the work himself and forgot his things?

No, that didn't make sense. Fine, he left them there as loaners and the card was so I knew who to return them to.

Once I had the boards down, I'd give him a call to have him pick up his property. This would give me plenty of time to figure out where to go to purchase my own things. No point in anyone thinking I was a thief because I kept this stuff forever. Oh no, I wasn't ever again going down the road of giving the rumor mill any fodder. Been there, done that, and gotten whacked in the process.

After I had a quick breakfast of a granola bar and juice box, I got to work. My first task of the day and my biggest priority: attack the windows with all my might. Which turned out to be no small feat. But I can exert much more force than most people think is possible from taking one glance at me. I'm five foot nothing and weigh something like a hundred pounds soaking wet. Never forget dynamite comes in small packages.

Hence, before long, half the boards were down, lying half-hidden in the grass. The now-revealed grimy glass did its best to wink back at me in the morning sunlight. Not a pane broken that I could tell, but more than a few cracked seals and damaged frames. All fixable problems with the right tools and a little patience. As I leaned into my fifth or sixth window, my new friend showed up.

"Hey ya, sup!" Hank yelled from the bottom of the ladder. I almost fell off, lost deep in thought about how best to twist my body and not kill myself.

A sheet of plywood weighs about half of what I do, so trying to keep it on a wall with half the screws out wasn't the easiest of tasks. Well, if you're foolish to try to do so alone, that is.

"One second," I responded as I dropped a screw or ten from my mouth. I shifted my weight a fraction to glance down from my perch. Yeah, I shouldn't have been putting old rusty bits of metal between my teeth. But I didn't have enough hands to do otherwise with them. I'm rather talented, if I must say so myself. However, I'm no octopus.

Hank, without prompting, climbed the ladder behind me, reaching up for the bottom of the board I had half off. Well, this did make things a whole lot simpler. I no longer needed to lean onto the wood to keep it in place while contorting in a rather awkward way to use the screwdriver. "Thanks," I stated as a few bits of dust rained down on him.

"No biggie." He grunted as he put his back into holding up the heavy board.

When we finished with the rest of the windows, I offered to order a pizza for lunch. "Na, burga's betta." He whapped me on the back. "I know a place." His open-mouthed grin showed off his white teeth with a hint of a gap between his two upper front ones.

Choking from the pounding I'd received the second before, "Well, I gotta call the guy who left the ladder first so he can come grab it. Oh, and make sure it's cool if I keep the other tools for a little bit longer. Fine by you?"

"Na, ya can't call him. He don't want no stuff back. He don't work no more." Hank started to stroll out of the yard.

"Wait!" I rushed to grab my purse, lock the door, and then catch up to him. "He left his card. Why would he do that if he doesn't work?"

"Oh, dat some other dude. Not as good. But might do right by ya." He chuckled as he continued to amble down the street. His arms dangled at his sides. His blue shorts threatened to slide down to his ankles and his pink t-shirt went dark red in spots from the sweat stains.

I frowned. "I don't understand." I needed some clarification here; this wasn't adding up somehow.

"My pal let me help him some with odd jobs for a bit. But hadn't seen him long since. Is okay. He don't live round here. Ya need help. So I call him to see what he be up to. Thought he might do the job. He said no. But dat he got some stuff might help ya." He nodded as if this explained everything. Yet, it didn't.

"Oh, well, thanks for trying. Most of the work I think I can do myself." I patted him on the arm. So, I guess the mystery man was going to remain a mystery.

He snorted. "No way, lady. You all pasty, small and a girl. I be a man now. I help. Yup." He thumped his chest, bold as could be.

While I do believe he'd meant this as a question, it'd come out as a statement. But the put-down and slam because of my race, gender, and size wasn't necessary. I'm stronger than I appear both inside and out. And color never has anything to do with anything as far as I was concerned.

We continued to walk up the street a few blocks before turning left. With the sun burning down on us, I wished I'd grabbed a hat. Not sure how much help it would've been. I ended up drenched in sweat from head to toe like I'd hopped out of the shower two seconds ago. So much so, I started to squish as I walked along. Best way to describe the situation – swampy. Don't think the different weather crossed my mind at all when I first decided to move out here. There's a big difference between being near the ocean versus in the mountains. I'd always lived in what's considered a high mountain desert. Rain was smelled, not felt, more often than not. Virga is such a wonderful thing.

So, you can imagine my happiness that after a few blocks we stopped before a little dive burger joint. And a very popular one at that. People milled around everywhere. Sitting on cars, at tables, on benches, and standing on the sidewalk. All were munching on burgers and fries, sipping their drinks, and chatting. Unlike me, it seemed they didn't mind the sizzling heat and humidity. Do think I would've killed for some AC about then. But it wasn't to be. This place didn't have indoor seating. Nope, the building wasn't much more than a shed with two openings carved into it. One almost appeared too small to walk through though it had to be the door. The other nothing more than the window counter for taking orders. Cluttered with napkins, straws, lids, and other paraphilia necessary for this type of establishment.

Hank strolled through the crowd, greeting many with a fist bump here or a handshake there. Once at the takeout window, he took the lead and ordered for us. "Her dough." He hooked his thumb over his shoulder at me.

I paid, all the while ignoring the stares. Several people got up from a nearby table, and Hank claimed it, swiped at it with a napkin. "No whites here most days," he said as he plopped down in the plastic lawn chair.

As I sank into my own seat, I gave a sly peek around. Yup, he was correct in his assertion. Brown, black, latte perhaps, but nothing pale as a new moon like me.

A flash of my old neighbor, Mrs. Diaz, floated through my mind. She was the first immigrant I'd ever known. Hum. I think those in her family might be the only people I'd ever met who weren't from this country. She hailed from Mexico, and I never did quite figure out how she and her husband found themselves but a few feet from Canada.

Over the years, a few other minorities popped into my life. Let's see now, who else? Ah, my dear friend Ike. Well, he wasn't someone I should've ever been close to for so many reasons. Yet, to this day, I missed those conversations of ours. Nope, I couldn't recall any others. Whoa! Kinda pathetic of me to never have sought out diversity. However, to be fair, I grew up in an area of my home state where few outsiders dared to set foot. There wasn't much there. For the most part, we all looked and acted the same. But here was different. And that was good. I needed something unlike what I believed "normal" to look like.

"So, tell me more about Miss Samuel and her brother. And what happened in my house." I turned to look at my companion, wanting some tit for tat. I'd shared something about me, so now was his turn to spill some dirt.

"Oh, don't know much 'bout dat. Long 'fore I got born, ya know." He nodded, tapping his fingers on the table and rocking his chair a little. The plastic legs bent, and he started to wobble to one side before planting the feet hard on the ground again. "She'll tell ya 'bout it, no prob." He bobbed his head, giving me a wee grin. "She likes talkin'."

"Alright. How do I find her?" I sighed. He wasn't being much help here. Teases me with a wild tale of murder and then no follow-through.

"Later. Now, we eat at ya place. Ya need to keep me up on ya tale." He laughed, slapping the table, making it jump. "You funny lady."

I wasn't sure if he felt embarrassed being with this little old white lady. Or if he thought my story wasn't fit for public consumption. Either way, I didn't feel the urge to argue. But this posed another problem and one more thing I wanted to buy sooner rather than later. Outdoor table and chairs. The stairs were too uncomfortable, plain and simple. Which meant I needed to hop on the internet tonight to shop for things and have them shipped directly to my house. And then pray the driver would deliver to what for all the world looked like an abandoned shack.

Deep breath. Don't work yourself into a lather over things that are difficulties for another day.

When a young woman from the café brought over our bag of food and a tray of drinks, Hank hopped up. He took everything without looking at me and started to take slow strides back the way we came. Upon our return to my house, we again sat on the steps for a lack of anywhere better. The sun had shifted so a hint of shade had appeared on that side of the house. As an added plus, a faint breeze now moved the moist air a little. Didn't help much, but I appreciated every tiny bit.

We sat for a while, munching on our lunch. Hank inhaled everything he touched, while I surveyed the clouds floating across the sky.

"Spill already, lady!" Hank jerked on my arm, looking up at me as he took a long pull on his soda.

"Not sure I want to tell you more. You don't seem to take me seriously." I took another bite of my burger.

"Ah, ya like my ma. I made her mad too." He looked down at his dirty, worn sneakers. "She hate me."

Ouch, that hit a bit too close to home. Paul had screamed, "You hate me!" during our final fight. "Oh, honey, all kids feel that about their parents at some point. But you have to know it's almost never true. For the most part, even when parents look like they're angry, they still love the stuffing out of their kids." I gave his arm a squeeze, tapping his chin so he would turn his eyes up toward me rather than the ground.

"Ya sure?" He bit his thumbnail, the gesture of an unsure child wanting nothing more than to be wrapped in a giant hug after scraping his knee.

"Well, most of the time. I know it's true of me." My words were the only form of embrace I could give him; anything more would be highly inappropriate. "So, moving forward, don't treat me like some old doddering fool. Cool?"

"Wha ya mean?" He tilted his head, scratching at the back of his neck a bit.

"What I'm telling you is the truth, not some joke from a TV show." I tapped on the step to make my point.

"Cool." A grin crept over his face.

"Okay, let me see, where did I leave off…." I cocked my head, thinking of what I'd already said. I didn't want to repeat myself.

"Ya bounced when he won't." Hank gave this simple statement as he dug into the bag of food, coming up with a fistful of fries.

"Ah, yes. Well, as I see now, that wasn't the best decision to have made." As I once again began to take a walk down memory lane, a flood of emotions washed over me. The path of my life had gone in such a different direction because of that day. To a place I'd never seen coming.

Chapter 8

As I dragged my feet across the landing, down the stairs, through the parking lot to my car, I debated my next move. And by that I want you to understand, I mean in the literal sense. As in, where should my next home be? No way could I return to my apartment. My apartment I had worked so hard for and still couldn't afford without major sacrifices. My dear, sweet, insane hubby was welcome to it. To heck with the cleaning deposit and my excellent credit. They weren't worth the kind of effort required to put up with Tom. I needed to escape again. Living in my car sounded like a tempting option right about then. Tom wouldn't be able to find me ever again if I didn't have an address, right?

Laying on the hood of my car for a moment, the cool metal on my face felt like a slap. Bringing my real world and all of the complications in my life back into sharp focus. What must the neighbors think of me now? First, men's clothing strewn about and now me hugging my car like my life depended on it. My life nothing more than a catastrophe.

My marriage had turned into a series of one-night stands. Wait, could you say that when nothing had ever happened? And I do mean nothing … not even a kiss. Well, there was that peck on the cheek at the wedding. And no, I guess you couldn't count last night – whatever that was – a one-night stand. Nor could you count the first night either, since we were together for, what, an hour or so in his truck? Oh, but then again, I'd seen him naked. That had to count for something. What a few glimpses of your nude spouse meant I didn't have complete clarity on. But based on my feelings in the heat of the moment, it wasn't good.

Sure, my life and marriage weren't pretty to look at. I worked too hard. I studied too much. And my marriage was supposed to have been left behind in my tiny town when I moved. Yet here it was, rearing its ugly head in the form of a husband/burglar/vandal. Yikes.

My parents had instilled in me from a very young age to roll with the punches. They never made any disaster seem like it was any big deal – the new-to-them car got totaled? Oh well, they had bought the cheapest one on the used car lot in the first place. The roof of the cabin leaked because of the worst hailstorm in a hundred years? Oh well, it was time to replace the roof anyway.

You get where I'm going with this, right? This whole mess with Tom needed some creative problem solving was all. I needed to do as the song said, "But if you love him, you'll forgive him, even if he's hard to understand…. Stand by your man." Phoning the police and reporting his crimes didn't feel like the right thing to do. I'd made a commitment here; this was my mess to fix somehow.

But at the moment, I wasn't up to that task or any other. All I was capable of was trying not to cry while hanging onto my car for dear life. My emotions were boiling over, and I never used to have any feelings about anything. Calm and steady was my general mood before I'd met Tom.

Straightening myself up to a half-leaning position, I looked up at my door with my chin cupped in my hand. I couldn't run away from my obligations. As a student. As an employee. Or as a wife. I'd made a sacred bond before God and man – for better or worse.

Yet, when the first opportunity had arisen back home, I'd taken off like a rocket. Pretended I didn't have a plus-one when I landed here. Never mind that was beside the point. I'd received the marriage certificate in the mail. It had the official seal of approval from the state on it. We were as married as it gets. Yes, I'd wanted to burn the cursed certificate and pretend the thing wasn't real the moment I ripped open the envelope in utter disgust.

But that wouldn't have changed a thing. Our marriage was all legal and binding, forever and a day. No going back. I was the better and he was the worse in this equation. So, hi-ho, hi-ho, it's off to work I go. Someone had to support the two of us. From the little knowledge I had about my beloved, there was no way he would ever wear the pants in this relationship. You can take that to mean whatever you like – it worked on so many levels.

I'll spend the day pondering how to help or find help for my husband. Nodding to myself, I felt this was the best I could do at the moment.

Sliding into my car, another thought hit me. People would see him around so my marriage secret was exposed now, I guess. I'd have to tell people. Oh, the joy. Oh, the horror. To have to face people and say, "Listen, this may sound a little weird, but I'm married." Like to everyone at my school. Like to my co-workers. Like to everyone in my church. Like to my neighbors.

Like to my landlord. Might want to wait on telling him. He would have a cow about the damage to the apartment. It's possible I'd end up evicted and wind up living in my car whether I desired to or not. Not a comforting thought, what with my car being a VW Bug and all. It wasn't much bigger than my bed.

I wished I'd dipped into my emergency stash of chocolate before I'd fled home. My stomach grumbled in response to the grinding of the motor as the engine roared to life. But the emotional hole I'd fallen into was too deep for something as basic as chocolate to fill. A migraine washed over me with giant waves of pain and nausea. Forget my plan from a second ago. Time to call in sick, find a quiet little spot, and ignore life for a while.

Reaching into my glove box for my emergency stash of migraine meds, I began to pray. About my life, for my husband, and for my marriage. Yes, I should've done this in that brief week before my wedding day. But prayer, like all those important questions, had never entered my mind. No, it had all been a matter of getting out of my parents' house. About no longer being controlled and doing my own thing for a while.

Consequently, God had slipped by unnoticed in those dizzying few days. Even after my wedding day, I hadn't prayed about my marriage. I had listened to the sermons to discover some guidance for my life, yes. But prayer, no. For the simple reason, nothing remotely marital had happened. These two people hadn't become one. Being alone made me almost forget somewhere out in the universe another half of me now existed. Oh, heavens yes, I should've been praying fervent prayers for the safe and speedy return of my wayward spouse. Yet, I remained silent for months.

Dry swallowing one of the huge pills, my throat closed tight and I coughed in a painful fit. I pulled out of the parking lot as I continued to choke for a few minutes more. *Dear Lord, please don't let me be misunderstood. By You, by anyone. I was only trying to do what everyone expected of me. I've blown it big time, I know. Who can I turn to? Who can I trust?* My fingers began a slow tap on the wheel. The ticking hurt my head, and I stopped. My eyes squinted in tight, so much so that driving became difficult.

Debated about calling in sick or making some kind of effort to be responsible. I cringed at the very thought of work. In the end, I felt I wasn't ready to face any more "real" life today. Being an adult sucked. My parents had always made everything look so easy, like water flowing downhill. No resistance whatsoever. What could their secret be? Why was I such a failure? I'd only been an adult for a few months and had made more blunders than they ever had. Could things end up being much worse than right at this moment? Yikes, I dreaded the answer and hoped for my sake the answer was no.

Stopping at the convenience store around the corner, I called work on the payphone. Hated to call in sick, but my boss was beyond understanding when I said I had a wicked migraine. She was great about things like that. Then I entered the store and stocked up on munchies. With a sigh of relief, I took off for the beach at the lake forty-five minutes away. Being the middle of winter, I knew I'd find the place deserted and all mine. No one is insane enough to sit on the beach in the northwest during this time of year. Except me. I craved solitude, nothing more, and wasn't caring in the least about the weather. Buildings began to fade as the trees became more prevalent. Then the trees became thinner as I neared the lake. Rolling down the window, the smell of the sweet air of the water, pine, and moss rushed into the car.

By now, the meds had kicked in. The drummer in my head had gone from banging a humungous bass drum to a homemade cardboard oatmeal can. The light almost didn't hurt my eyes anymore, my squint now smaller. The road before me no longer appeared as a small pinpoint that was impossible to focus on.

And I started to wonder if I should listen to some music. In the end, I felt it pushed my luck to bring in any extra sound and kept the car silent. The slap of the tires and the wind whistling in the now open window were the only racket. Why was white noise so soothing while music could make a headache worse? I guess because the drummer in your head can bang in time to the music. And that wouldn't be great.

Grabbing the donuts from the grocery bag, I wolfed them down during the last few miles until the cutoff for the beach. My nausea was almost gone by the time I finished them. As I got close to being human again, I looked forward to a day at my secret spot. I'd found this little out-of-the-way place far off the beaten track by accident. About a month after I'd moved all the way across the state to start my new life of freedom, I'd wandered here.

Needing a place of solitude, after a bad day at school and work, I'd hopped in my car. Then I drove around until I'd become so lost that no one would ever be able to find me again. Down several dirt roads, round one too many corners, hidden behind the trees. All because I wanted nothing and found nothing in return. But I'd discovered this tiny little beach in the end. White sand, a few pebbles, and curved around a small cove. By some small miracle, I'd figured out how to make my way back to the highway on that day. And had kept coming back on many of my days off ever since. No, I wasn't alone every time I went back in the late summer and fall. But for the most part, they were people like me who were seeking the silence and so left me in peace.

I was in luck, and it wasn't snowing on this day. The sun shone bright in the winter sky, not a cloud from horizon to horizon. The expected high in the lower fifties. The nip of a sudden gust biting the exposed skin of my calves reassured me I would remain alone. As I neared the dark water, I dropped my shopping bags of treats and rolled up my coat as a pillow. Sinking down to the sand, I curled my bare legs into my skirt as best I could. So glad it was a long one in a heavy knit, and I had on a thick sweater. Still and all, goosebumps covered me until my body became adjusted to the chill.

The waves crashed onto the shore, leaving an off-white foam and debris of leaves and twigs behind. The high whitecaps were bright dots against the blue sky. Birds dipped into the water to fish for their snacks. The gentle breeze cool despite being so close to the earth, but I was beyond caring about anything. Don't think it took long for the view and the sun to lull me into a deep sleep. Best thing for me after the long night and morning I'd endured with Tom.

Crunch, crunch, crunch. Rolling over, my eyes came unglued a millimeter at a time. Not ready to be awake and face anything other than the back of my eyelids, I groaned. Sleeping is wonderful, but whatever this was couldn't be. Not with the way my life was going at the moment. Almost certain some kind of wild animal had gotten into my food. And I didn't own a gun, because when I'd moved out of my parents' house, I'd told them hunting wasn't for me anymore. My bad. My trigger finger itched. It knew how to handle this type of situation without blinking an eye.

"Ah, you're awake then. Ike hoped you didn't mind but Ike started on lunch because Ike was hungry. Ike didn't know how long you were going to sleep," this bear of a man at my side said as my eyes flew open at the words.

I should've freaked, yet I didn't. I wanted to shake myself hard or move out of the spot I laid in. But it didn't make sense to scare the giant by screaming or jumping up and running off. For some reason, I didn't believe he'd hurt me.

He wore a jacket more multi-colored patches than coat. His blue jeans so stained that calling them blue was a stretch. His long white hair wild around his head, like he'd stuck his finger in a socket and shocked himself. His skin so black that his eyes and teeth looked as if they were much whiter than I'm sure they were. I couldn't tell how old he might be, but I do believe he was somewhat older than my parents were and much too old to be homeless. Or at least I hoped so. You wouldn't want your grandfather to be homeless, now, would you?

"Ike is me, in case you forgot who you invited to dine with you." He pointed first to his chest then to his head with one of his massive sausage fingers.

Well, it's a blessing he'd told me his name since I hadn't invited him. Or ever set eyes on him before.

They don't have homeless people in my small hometown. Or if they do, they're so hidden from sight I never had a clue they existed. My mother made it clear to me when I left for the "big" city that most of "those" people were criminals. You know, the homeless or poor or odd-looking sorts. They did drugs. They beat their kids. They jaywalked. They littered. They chewed gum. While I was to help "those" people, it was in the sense of watching out for them. You never knew what they might do. As the Good Book says, 'we are to be sheep in the midst of wolves; so be as wary as serpents, and as innocent as doves'.

Good grief, who am I kidding? This morning, I woke up to my naked husband sleeping in my living room. After he'd broken into my apartment. Plus, he was higher than a kite, and he'd destroyed my kitchen. I was a lamb who was about to be slaughtered at home. I guess I'm safe having lunch with a homeless gentleman on a beach in the freezing cold.

Yeah, I know. Being a woman of virtue, I shouldn't have considered staying for a second. As a married woman, being anywhere alone with another man was akin to having an affair. Right? Yet, we were out in the open for anyone who happened to pass by to see. Still, who was gonna see me way out here in the middle of nowhere? Our clothes were on. I was good.

My head swam, trying to decide the best course of action. *Stay, go, stay, go?*

In the end, everything boiled down to one thing. My mother. Let's face it, when your mother starts drilling you before you can walk, things become habits. Habits you can't shake. Even when you try as hard as you can or move to the other side of the planet. You've got this stuff you're stuck doing on autopilot. Like saying please and thank you even when you aren't thankful. Or despite the fact you don't want what you're offered. Like cilantro. Or calling someone sir or ma'am when you don't respect them any more than you would respect a thief. Yup, they could be the biggest idiot you've ever met, but according to my parents, they still deserve the title. These things are part of your nature, who you are. Well, this me in all my glory. This is what my mother did to me. Turned me into someone who's polite to a fault. I betcha you don't see people like that every day. No, most people are flat-out rude and are proud they are.

After this brief war in my head, being civil won. I pasted on a grand smile and rolled with the tide of the moment. Because this is what I'm an expert at, skating through life and hoping for the best. Bruises heal. Well, at some time in the far distant future they will. Most of the time.

"I'm Amy. You're welcome to eat anything you like." My words weren't reaching my ears; the thumping in my chest drowned them out. "I have a generous assortment of goodies for you to choose from. I'm sorry that none are homemade, but still, these items should prove more than satisfactory." Waving my shaking hand toward the grocery sacks, my beaming face set in stone.

Yet another thing my mother trained me to be: the perfect hostess. When all else fails, throw a tea party. Not kidding about that. She's famous for her tea parties, cucumber sandwiches and all. Didn't matter if we had running water or electricity at our house or not. The church ladies were always welcome. Or the guys who came to help with the harvest every year. Or anyone else who happened by.

Not wanting to spook the guy, I sat up as slow as I could. The super-size bag of potato chips lay half-hidden beside Ike's tree trunk of a leg. The bag now flat, like those chips had given their lives for the cause. The bottle of my favorite iced tea flopped over on its side nearby, half-buried in the sand. Also empty.

"What got such a pretty little thing like you so upset?" He dug through a shopping bag, coming up with one of the king-size candy bars. He began to eat it wrapper and all. Watching in fascinated horror, I waited for him to spit the bits of wrapper out. He never did, swallowing everything in giant gulps. His Adam's apple bobbed up and down, and his tongue licked his lips to find every speck of chocolate and nougat. Disgusting.

"Um..." My fingers squished the sand, in and out. Trying in vain to ground myself in reality, I focused on each digit, one at a time as I moved them. Yet, the cold, wet sensation running through my fingers didn't help make the moment real. Or to make me feel like I'm living in the present. *I'm still asleep and dreaming; wake up, wake up!*

"No need to act shy. Only one reason anyone invites Ike to lunch. To tell Ike things they can't tell anyone else. Because Ike won't ever tell. Ike knows loose lips sink ships. Yes, dear. Ike knows everyone's secrets. Ike knew about John and Marilyn before anyone else. As in Kennedy, you know." He gave me the sweetest smile.

My knotted stomach began to untwist. Something about him was lovable and comfortable. Almost like having a conversation with my favorite stuffed teddy bear; don't ask me why. I wanted to squeeze the stuffing out of him and never let go. And these feelings were washing over me despite the wads of wrapper stuck in the huge gaps of his teeth.

"So, tell Ike what's got you so upset, lovey." He patted down his hair with a quick swipe of his large paw and tugged at the front of his coat. It looked for all the world like he was trying to make himself more presentable. As if he was doing everything he could to get down to business. Or prove himself worthy of my time.

Taking in as much air as possible, my whole body tensed before I let the breath out, "I married a guy after only going on one date. Turns out he's a dope-smoking, naked hippie. Plus, he believes in crazy conspiracy theories, like how the government spies on everyone. Oh, and he's a momma's boy too. Turns out he lived at her house. I don't know what to do."

What was I doing? This information was something I should've been sharing with my pastor. Or a half-decent marriage counselor. Or at the very least my mother. Not some homeless guy on the beach who thought he could talk to dead presidents and actresses. But he was here, and for some reason, he felt safe. Maybe he'd be able to understand Tom better than anyone else. After all, they were on the same wavelength – so far out in left field they'd left everyone else behind as they alone wandered in a world of their own creation and design. It didn't matter. The important thing was to release this burden somehow.

"Oh, but you do, child. Your heart has already told you what to do. You just didn't listen. And why was that?" He patted my knee and half my leg with his giant hand. The rough leather of his skin grated my skin even through my thick knit skirt. Those hands had seen a lot of tough years, done a lot of hard work.

Then he began to rummage in the bag and pulled out another candy bar. Again, he ate it wrapper and all. And again, I couldn't turn away from the dreadful sight. Like watching a train wreck in slow motion. You don't want to watch as each car goes flying off the rails, knowing someone will be hurt. But you still feel you must witness the carnage for some strange reason.

Turning my head to stare at the lake for a few minutes, I wondered why this stranger touching me wasn't a big deal. However, it horrified me beyond measure when my husband tried to.

Because this stranger is not tied to you, not connected to you. It doesn't mean anything more than a simple gesture of friendship. Still, it should've burned or hurt me in some way. I should've wanted to be a faithful wife, and now I could never say this was true. I'd allowed another man to touch me. So what if he was a lot older and it hadn't meant anything to him? My brain clicked. My husband and I both were guilty of destroying our marriage. And my part of the blame went far beyond me sitting here with this man or allowing him to have his hand on me.

Looking back at Ike, I fiddled with my hair for a moment, twirling the strands around my finger. "You're right; I didn't listen to myself. I just got so angry. I've never shown him even an ounce of love or compassion. I only looked out for myself. Marriage is forever. My father told me I had to keep my commitment, but I just didn't care about that at all. Oh boy, I should've stayed at home this morning and tried to help him. I debated about what the best thing to do, for a second but didn't act on my thoughts. I came here instead. It's my duty now, my job. I'm the worst wife ever."

Hanging my head, I gazed down at my fingernails, dirty from the sand. My heart was as unclean as my hands in so many ways. It took most of my effort to not start sobbing and never stop. It'd been wrong of me to be so upset with Tom. He'd shouted a cry for help, something taught to me since I was in diapers to never ignore. My parents had their faults but they were there when the chips were down. No matter what you'd done. And no matter who you were.

Yet, I didn't want to support the one person in my own house who needed so much. Shame on me. I was better than that...well I should've been better than that. I wasn't following what the Bible said, 'Do not merely look out for your own personal interests, but also for the interests of others.'

"Well, deary, tell him the government took you in for questioning since he believes in that sort of thing." Ike roared in a deep belly rumbling sort of laugh. And I joined in with an almost hysterical howl of my own. He looked at me and added, "Oh, but that would never work. They're spying on him, not you, right?"

We both laughed louder, deeper, harder. Each of us holding our sides, lost in the moment.

Regaining my composure for a second, I said, "So true. I never asked for more information about the whole spying thing. The only thing I know for sure is they've got bugs in the smoke detectors. How ridiculous is that?" That released the floodgates, and I laughed so hard I started to snort. Then I gasped for breath as the tears began to flow.

My face soon became wet from my tears and snot dripping from my nose. Not sure if I cried to cry, or cried because of laughing so hard. Either way, it felt wonderful. I continued to chortle until no breath remained in me and fell back over onto the cool sand. Blinking hard at the brightness of the sun, I tried to regain my composure. Not worried in the least about how puffy my eyes were. My breaths were labored, raspy and painful as I coughed several times.

Ike said nothing more. Standing up, he leaned over me and kissed the top of my head. Then he gave me a simple smile and waved at me. I gazed up at him as he picked up all of my shopping bags and started to meander up the beach. I should've stopped him since he took both my lunch and dinner, but I let him be. Let him have his reward for his sage advice. Love the unlovable. Even if the unlovable is your husband.

Chapter 9

"Ah, lady, now I know ya's telling tales." Hank sprawled on the grass, laughing so hard I was sure his sides were splitting. "Ya didn't see some weird homeless Yoda. Ya dreamt him up!"

"Fine, make fun of me if you must. My life is my life. I'm not going to change the truth for some kid I'd met a heartbeat ago." Or maybe my memory wasn't as outstanding as I thought it was. But no doubt about it, Ike was as real as the wonderful burger I'd gulped down for lunch.

"Sorry." He sat up on his elbows.

"Enough for today," I announced. "I've got lots of chores to do. And don't you have some school work you need to finish?" I gave him a swift scowl.

"Na. I done with dat." He stood up and began picking up the debris of our meal. "I help guys with odd jobs some. My granddaddy don't want no trouble." His shoulders were tight, his head down.

Behind these words lurked something, but this wasn't the time to ask what. Right at that moment, I could feel the anger rolling off his back. I'd wait for a time when he felt relaxed and calm before making an attempt to pry into what was an obvious sore spot.

"Which is why you're hanging out with this old lady?" It was my turn to chuckle and shake my head as I scrutinized him in my yard. He was a lost boy instead of a lost cat or dog, but still, this was something I'd gotten great at over the years – loving the unlovable or the unloved. Turned out, I had more in common with people like that than the "normal" people. But then again, there's nothing normal about anyone. I tried a different approach. "Okay then. How much have you learned about remodeling a house?" While my initial desire had been to do this project alone, every inch of me cried out that I needed to help this boy. For whatever reason, we'd been thrown together – for better or for worse.

"Plenty, I be good to ya." He spun his head toward me, face lit up and eyes wide.

"I'll provide the food and pay you every Saturday. You make sure it's okay with your grandfather, deal?" I held out my hand to shake on the contract.

"Yup!" His sweaty, greasy hand clasped mine tight.

"See you tomorrow then." I watched him hurry off down the street, his arms swinging at his side. I'd made his day with the offer of a job.

After his reaction to my story, I kept my mouth shut for several days as we worked side by side on the house. He showed me where a local hardware store was which offered free delivery. Major score. He led me to the local post office and waited as I filled out the form to have mail delivered at a "dead" address. Don't get me started on my feelings about that moniker for my house.

He also pointed out a small coffee shop nearby, a place to hang out in air-conditioned comfort any time I wanted to. Plus, have my breakfast at every day. Coffee and a pastry were so much better than whatever I would've been able to scrounge up. And in between these errands, we began to clean, prep, and repair the house. The process slow, each task leading to a new problem or ten. However, I wasn't in any rush.

I started calling around to receive estimates for the major work. The roofers came, the plumbers came, and the electricians came. All shook their heads and asked me why. Not why I required that work. No, that was plain for all to see. Rather, why I moved to this little corner of the world in the first place. And why wasn't I staying in a pleasant, cozy motel while the work got done.

But I didn't share tidbits of my life with any of them. Not how I'd ended up here. Or why I was comfortable without what most people considered to be the necessities of life. No, the only things I need were air, water, and food. Everything else were luxuries to me, things I didn't need or want in my life. Not anymore.

If I stuck to my plan of doing as much of the work on my own as possible it'd take months to turn my little disaster into a gem. Not that I minded; I had all the time in the world. There were no longer any other responsibilities in my life. Being frugal for years had its upside, I'd retired at a very young age. My penny pinching and refusal to ever have debt of any kind had left me with a very tidy sum. Adding that money to what I received from a rather quick sale of my last house, I had more than enough to live on without ever working another day in my life. Who needed the government handout of social security? Not I. Sure, I'd take the few dollars Uncle Sam might throw my way when my time came many years from now. I wasn't stupid enough to look a gift horse in the mouth.

"I can't be here 'morrow," Hank rubbed his neck, rolling his head from side to side.

We'd ended late on that Saturday; we'd begun to put everything away from another long day of back-breaking work. We both were beyond tired, dirty and disheveled.

"No problem. You've been so helpful this week. Frankly, I'm surprised you showed up every day so far. You deserve a day off." I nodded at him, giving him a grin as I took the tools he handed to me so I could put them away.

"My granddaddy say to invite ya to church. We sing good, loud." His head bowed as he shuffled his feet on the rough subfloor. A cloud of dust began to rise around him. "Then to our pad for lunch after." He fiddled with his fingers.

"Sorry. I don't do church anymore." Quick as I could, I turned my back on him.

A tear formed in my eye and a lump in my throat. No, I wasn't going to sob like a baby in front of him or anyone, not after how people had treated me back home. No one had understood me then. Everyone was so horrified by me and what I'd become. By what I'd done. The door to the church got nailed shut as far as I was concerned.

"Ah, but ya such a nice lady. Ya must believe in something. Ya fed me all week. And today ya gave me a wad of cash and ya trust me with ya key. Ya said ya had faith in ya tale…" He put his hand on my shoulder, trying to pull me around to face him.

"That was then. No longer. Don't ask me again." I wasn't budging, my feet cemented to the floor and my heart heavy behind its solid as iron wall.

"Alrighty then. Monday, ya gotta tell me more. Or I gonna bring my granddaddy here to bring hellfire and brimstone down on ya." He chuckled as he patted my arm before taking long lopping strides out the open door.

Perfect. That was the last thing I needed. My stomach twisted into a painful knot, my head pounding as the blood rushed in. No way would I allow anyone on this planet to drag me screaming and kicking back into religion. I'd put that behind me long before I fled to this place. Along with everything else I'd once consider important. Without thinking, I punched out toward the wall. My knuckles bounced off an exposed stud. Leaving me wanting to swear like a sailor at the white-hot lightning shooting up my arm.

Ugh, this I didn't need. Not church, not broken fingers, none of it. Grabbing my purse, I locked the door behind me. With the swiftness of a person whose pants were on fire, I dashed down the street the few blocks to the local coffee shop. All the while, I cradled my hand against my chest as I cursed myself for being so stupid. As I rounded the last corner where the shop was, I heard music.

No, no, no. The place was cram-packed with people listening to a jamming live band. All I wanted was some ice, but that wasn't going to be easy. Rolling my eyes so far into the back of my head it hurt, I pursed my lips. Wishing for all the world I had electricity and a fridge so I could be at home with an ice pack right at this moment, I pushed open the door with much more force than required. It bounced against the wall.

And the sound of worship music assaulted my ears. Good gravy! The band played music normally reserved for church services. Nothing I wanted more at that second than to weep in anguish and run home. But my hand had started to swell, and the ache now almost unbearable. Others had drinks and food, and the baristas were behind the bar, so I hoped I could still buy what I needed.

Marching those few steps felt like an obstacle course. Tilting my head a little, yup, I'd heard the song before. Trying to block it out at the deafening level it was being played at wasn't possible.

Thus, I did my best to think of anything else. The beach at the lake, my son, anything. And then the counter stood in front of me with a smirking young man staring at me from behind it. Blowing out my breath, I stated as loud as I could, "Hi, this is gonna sound weird, but I hurt my hand and I need some ice in a bag."

Oh, of course, the song ended right as I started to speak so everyone in the place heard my declaration. Yup, at least half a dozen people whipped around toward me and piped up, "Want me to pray with you?" or something to that effect. I wanted nothing more than for the floor to open up and swallow me whole. This couldn't be happening, not now, not ever. Every inch of me recoiled, trying to curl into a ball and become as small as possible.

Without a word, the young man behind the bar grabbed some ice in a bag and passed it over. I'd been in the place maybe a minute or two, but by then, everyone was staring at me. Nothing else to do but straighten up my spine and walk out with my head held high. Giving a sort of princess wave, I strode toward the door. Someone opened it for me. My eyesight so blurry at that point from squinting I couldn't tell if the kind person was a man or woman. Once out of the building, I ran home, clutching my ice like I'd stolen a bag of gold.

So childish of me to have a panic attack over a bunch of people enjoying some silly music. But there it was. Somewhere in the back of my mind, I remembered seeing a notice at the shop about live music. It'd been taped on the door one of the mornings I'd dashed in for coffee. Bright pink, right there for everyone to see. However, I'd ignored it since I wasn't interested in anything but my project at home. I wasn't ever going to disregard those signs again. But I always missed warning messages. It's why I got in trouble as much as I did.

The next morning, as I lay in bed, my hand rested on the dusty floor, drumming out a beat. Was there another coffee shop close by? One tick of my fingernail, odds were no. This area didn't have much in the way of basic services. Another click or two on the rough wood and the lyrics to that feminist anthem popped into my head: "But it's wisdom born of pain. Yes, I've paid the price. But look how much I gained. If I have to, I can do anything. I am strong (strong) I am woman (invincible)."

Though, given my mood, I didn't bother to finish humming the song. Nope, I don't "roar." Never have. Go with the flow and hope for the best had always been more of my style. So, yeah, I didn't see myself going back to the place where I'd humiliated myself the night before. Wiggling a bit, I realized my mattress had deflated again. My butt had almost no cushion between it and the floor. Clearly, I couldn't lay here all day and mope. I was going to be uncomfortable and sore if I didn't get up and at least add some air to my bed. Oh, just wonderful. Whatever. I huffed out a giant sigh, biting my inner cheek. To heck with it. Hunger rumbled in my stomach, plus I needed a caffeine fix like nobody's business.

I got up and dressed, an ordinary day, nothing more, nothing less. All of those fine folks from the night before would be at church this morning, right? Right.

Nothing seemed amiss at the shop when I walked in. The same girl stood behind the bar as always. Same as every morning. Her hair pulled back into a ponytail, so blond it was white. Her tiny shape completely swallowed by the giant black apron she wore. I ordered and sat down by the window to watch the few people walking by. I worked my hand, wriggling my stiff fingers.

Fate had smiled on me it seemed; no major harm done from my foolish act. I'd brought my tablet so I could catch up on email or just fiddle on the internet for a while. My intention had been to do this in the evenings at home. But I was always so tired at the end of the day that as soon as I laid down, I fell into a deep sleep. The whole world could've blown up and I would've never known, I was so out of touch with everything anymore.

Don't know how long I'd parked myself there. My breakfast and coffee were long gone and still, I remained lounging by the window. And then someone sat down opposite me. I don't think I noticed at first. I had my headphones on, buried deep in some video at that stage. But my skin started to prickle, telling me I was being watched. Peeping up a tad over my reading glasses, I caught sight of male eyes drilling into me as he leaned forward in the chair. His black hair cut so short that he seemed bald. His eyes a piercing chocolate behind his wire-rimmed glasses. He wore a plain white buttoned-down shirt and black slacks. I was sure he'd come straight from church; thus, he was nothing but trouble. I know, I have issues.

"Hey," his voice a smooth baritone, "I was here last night and tried to catch you as you rushed out. No luck. So, uhm, how's the hand?" His smile rich and warm as he pointed to my hand. He blew over the top of his cup before taking a little sip of his drink, waiting for me to say something in reply.

No, just no. I wasn't going to have this conversation.

Option one: pretend I didn't hear a thing because of my headphones.

Option two: be rude and ignore the guy, plain and simple.

At this stage of my life, I was so beyond being polite that I didn't say please and thank you, for pity's sake. My mother would've given me a harsh scolding. And then sent me to my room for the rest of my life as punishment. Yeah, the good little girl I used to be hadn't been around for a very long time. There were so many reasons she got left behind. Well, to be honest, I'd killed that version of myself. And am quite happy I had.

He leaned even further toward me. "Okay, I get it. You don't talk to strangers. Fine. My name's Jessie. I've lived here my whole life and love motorcycles. I sometimes go to baseball games. See, now you know me. Er…" He hesitated when he still hadn't managed to get a response and I still refused to meet his eyes fully. He tapped his mouth with a finger, trying to think of what else to say to force me out of my shell.

He set his cup down on the side table and stood up. More than a tiny bit curious, I watched as he strode over to the bar. Motioned to the barista, tapped on the counter for a second. He said something I couldn't hear from that distance. A few minutes later, he made a giant show of picking up a new drink and walking back to my area with it.

"I got you another latte." He put the cup next to my empty one before sitting back down. All casual and at ease with himself, he crossed his slim legs, picked up his drink again, and took a slow sip. "Need anything else?"

Still, I said nothing but my eyes were darting back and forth. Locking onto the barista for a moment, she gave me a grin and the thumbs-up sign. Yup, after all these years of playing it safe, I'd landed in a rather awkward position. For it now appeared that all of my efforts of doing my best to ignore the world and stay out of harm's way had come down to this moment.

This man was one of those goody-two-shoes from some local church. Oh, goodness me. I had a complete understanding of those people and how they worked. They were the worst kind of people in the world and did the most damage. Glancing back at Jessie, I took off my readers with a slow, careful movement. I tapped them on my leg for a moment, still not uttering a sound.

He put his hands up in surrender as he cocked his head with a smirk and a click of his tongue. "Okay, another time then." He stood up; his lean frame highlighted by the light streaming in. "I'd really like to get to know you. So, I guess I'll see you around sometime." He gave me a quick salute. And with that, he left.

I blew out my held breath so hard my lips rattled. Every inch of my being a coiled-up spring waiting to pounce on... on something. I wasn't sure what. Oh, I so didn't need this. Not a man, not anyone religious, not anyone asking about my personal business. Clenching my hands into fists, I stopped for a moment. Trying to think of what made me the angriest about this whole incident with Jessie.

I almost snapped my fingers when the lightbulb went on. No one bought me anything, ever. I could provide for myself just fine, thank you very much. The drink was a major insult. Why had this jerk done this? Did I look like I needed a handout? No, I'm the one who gave to others, not the other way around. Rude. This guy was flat-out rude.

The man didn't know anything about me other than what he'd been able to see in our two brief encounters. But still, I didn't need this invasion into my life and private affairs. Couldn't he tell I was a clam in a shell? Closed up tight, nothing comes in or out?

Jumping up, I grabbed the cup he'd brought and my things. Shoving my tablet into my bag as quick as I could, my stomach churned in disgust at this whole episode. Tossed both my empty and his full cup in the trash as I made my way out, and as I did, a stone lifted off my chest. Breathing became easy again.

Chapter 10

On Monday, Hank showed up as I munched on a muffin and sipped on coffee. I sat at the outdoor table set which had arrived, as if by magic, first thing that morning. I'd gotten lucky and I'd heard the delivery truck's low rumble. The driver had slowed down but was about to drive off when I rushed outside. I'd been half awake and half-dressed. The guy still hesitated to unload even after I hurried out the door and signed for the package. He had stood there with his hand on the handle to the backdoor of the truck for much longer than needed.

Yup, I'd been right. People weren't wanting to leave valuables at an apparently abandoned house. Yet, I lived here in this house in all of its glory. No electricity, no running water, and no problems as far as I was concerned. I'd gone back to the simple life I should never have left. No, not the life I left a short time ago. Rather the one I'd left in my teens when I made the mistake of getting married. Funny, how I'd moved to the city to reunite with the basics. As in, all I need is food, water, and air. And I was going to keep telling myself this until my face turned blue so I would never forget again.

"Hey lady!" Hank strode up the sidewalk like he owned the place. His arms swinging by his side, a large brown paper sack in one.

"Hey, you, I've got an extra muffin or two. They had a special at the coffee shop this morning. Want one before we start today?" I stood, brushing the crumbs off my shorts as I did. Not like it mattered. My clothes were a disgusting mess.

"Naw. Lotta stuff leftover yesterday, brung ya some." He handed me the sack. "Church ladies be prayin' for ya." He nodded with a big goofy grin.

Oh, crud. Just what I didn't need, more people knowing my business. Or worse, anyone thinking they had the right to "pray" for me. Yeah, I recognized what *that* was code for: gossiping about someone. "Tell them not to worry. I'm fine, all right? I lived for years in a house with nothing fancy, so I'm used to it." I frowned. Busybodies were the last thing I wanted.

"Well, my granddaddy say the Good Book say, 'For I was hungry, and you gave me something to eat; I was thirsty and you gave me something to drink; I was a stranger, and you invited me in.' We'se just doin' dat." The beaming look on his face was enough to melt through the thickest of ice, maybe even this heart of mine.

And it more than surprised me that the verse had come out in perfect English, given his speech patterns. Then it hit me why his language was different. "You've done Bible quiz." I gave him a gigantic smile back. This is the event which has kids learning passages word for word exactly as written as part of a church team. Then having a game against other teams based on this knowledge.

"Sho' nuff." His mouth opened wide, his eyes twinkling. Then his face shut down as he took a look behind his back. "She keep yellin' to slow. But I walk fast." He shrugged his shoulders up to his ears.

Puzzled, I wondered who he was talking about as I didn't see anyone else on the street. "My son did Bible quiz as well." Trying to stay on track, I didn't want to worry about what or who might be coming around the bend. "He loved it; so much fun to see who'll win."

A flash of a younger version of Paul entered my mind. Him in his Sunday best, standing so proud and tall on the stage. Staring at the ceiling as he tried to wrap his mind around which passage might be the right answer to the question he'd been asked. Me biting my nails, holding my breath, and knowing I couldn't help him in any way.

Ignoring my comment, "Dat be her." He pointed to a figure coming around the nearest street corner. His face twisted a bit. His nose wriggled like he had an itch and he bounced on his heels.

A woman leaned heavy on a cane, taking each step with the care of someone walking on ice. Her dark ebony skin glowed against her light pink dress. Her white hair piled up into a high bun.

"You know her?" I rapped hard on the table with my knuckle. "Well, go help her before she topples over!" I gave a little chuckle and a shake of my head. Boys.

"Oh, fine." He snickered as he ambled to the old woman's side.

Sitting back down, I observed the pantomime before me. He took the small woman by her elbow, bending his head to say a word or two. She patted his hand, giving an answer back. With a small, measured gait, he guided her the rest of the way to my yard.

Once he had placed her into a chair with a light and gentle touch, I said, "Welcome, to my home. My name's Amy. You're my first official visitor." As I offered my hand to her, my stomach filled with butterflies.

This wasn't any way to entertain guests, I hadn't prepared anything at all. Oh, I do realize, it's not like I knew someone was coming to pay me a visit. But still, I needed to be better prepared for future callers. Cups, I needed cups. And plates. Ugh.

"Ah, yes. So I was told. I'm Miss Samuel. This used to be my home." She patted my hand with hers which had skin as soft as silk.

"Oh, of course! Hank told me there was a tragedy here and it's been vacant for years. You didn't have to come all this way to see me. I would've come to you if I'd known now was the right time. But thanks so much for doing so." I cringed inwardly at the effort this woman had made on my behalf. Golly, she looked like she was ninety going on six hundred. "Would you like something to eat, drink?"

Not like there was much – maybe a juice box, a muffin or two. But still, I had to ask. Politeness hadn't gone by the wayside forever. Or taken a complete detour.

"Oh, no thank you, dear. And it was no trouble at all to come here this morning. My doctor said I need to get my steps in. Helps keep my sugar under control." She chortled at this. "But as far as the tale of the house goes, that's a sad one." Her face tightened.

"Well, over thirty years ago I guess it was now, my only son, Anthony, got in with the wrong crowd. When he stole their money, he hid out with me. Now, I didn't know this or wouldn't have let the fool darken my door. Child or no. But it didn't take long before they found him and they came a calling. Praise God, I was at church or I'd have gone up to heaven that day as well. Every window shot out; the walls pitted. I came home to police everywhere, my son dead and my home destroyed." A finger ticked on the tabletop.

Her face turned grim as the memory washed over her. Her chin dropped to her chest as she closed her eyes tight. In a moment, her nostrils flared as she took a deep breath. Looking at me with her dark eyes shiny from tears not shed, she patted my hand a few times. "Still hurts even now, you know?" She dipped her head for a heartbeat or two.

Hmmm, son not brother, and the tale turned out to be much more sordid than Hank had let on.

"Yes, ma'am. I'm sorry for your loss." I felt like a heel for dredging up this woman's pain to feed my sense of curiosity. Hurt was something I was no stranger to.

"Well, I moved out. Found a cute little house nearby. Still wanted to be in the neighborhood with my friends and church, you know. Fixed up the outside of this house." She tipped her head toward the building. "Tried to sell it for years. No takers, until you."

She looked me right in the eye. "Oh, but the scavengers came, what with the house sitting empty for so long. Tore out the wiring to sell it for cash or so I hear. Later, the plumbing disappeared. Those vultures took the bathtub, gosh darn it, never did figure out how." She gave a tiny chuckle, with a little waggle of her head. "And now here you are and you're the right person to bring this shell of a home back to life."

Her gaze shifted back to the structure; I was sure she saw it as it had been. When her son was living. Heck, I'm sure when her son was a tiny thing *before* he got into a world of trouble.

She scanned it for some time before continuing. "The soul was ripped out of this place that morning when Anthony died. Do you understand?"

I do believe I understood more than she would ever know. Losing a child is the worst thing to ever happen to a parent. However, unlike her, I had the slim chance to make it right with my child somehow. He wasn't lost, only ignoring me, plain and simple. For reasons which were beyond my control. Still, there wasn't a whole lot I could do about it right at the moment. A tear developed in the corner of my eye. I dabbed at it with my finger in a rapid swipe, hoping no one noticed.

"Yes, ma'am," The only response possible for me to make. It sounded lame. But there wasn't any way I could say more without the floodgates opening. If I allowed one memory about my son out, it would start to chip away at the enormous wall straining to keep them all in. Then in the blink of an eye, all of my recollections would come rushing to the surface. The dam would burst; my emotions I worked so hard to never feel would be out and on display for all to see. Which would be very bad for everyone.

She struggled to rise; I touched her hand for a moment. "Thanks so much for coming. I'm glad you told me about the house. I hope to have you over again soon, proper-like next time."

She leaned over to kiss my forehead, "Goodbye, dear. God bless you and your efforts here." She wobbled, more than a bit unsteady on her feet.

Hank appeared from somewhere and grabbed her elbow to steady her. "Get ya home," he said as they began to walk toward the street. He towered over her as they shuffled along. I gazed at them until they were out of sight.

My body had become a lead weight burdened by Miss Samuel's words, making me unable to rise from my chair. Turning my glance, I sat there looking at my home with new eyes. Everything had shifted. This was no longer a slap-some-lipstick-on-the-pig kind of project. Nope, it'd turned into something much bigger. And this is what I needed most. I'd been a caterpillar in a chrysalis for too long. I needed to break out and turn into something. This house would change with me; we would emerge stronger together.

And Miss Samuel would be my first dinner guest when I finished. A noise behind me startled me out of my musing. Turning my head toward the street, I noted that Hank had returned. Apparently, I'd been lost in thought for quite some time.

"Wat we'se doing a-day?" He headed toward the house. "Beside ya tellin' me a tale." He chuckled as he peeked back at me. I still hadn't moved from my chair.

"Fine, I'll start the next chapter if I must…." I picked up the trash from my breakfast, not wanting to do much else. But my mouth, as if on autopilot, started spilling words out. "So, after I left the lake, things were better. The world now brighter somehow. Still, as it would turn out, that feeling was a bit premature on my part."

Chapter 11

Entering the parking lot of my apartment complex can be comforting on a normal day. My home felt like a safe harbor in this mixed-up world. But today, a sense of dread washed over me as I turned the corner. You know how it is – like you've swallowed rocks, and nothing is ever going to be right again. Or a tidal wave has hit you and you're downing, never to see the light of day again as you sink deeper and deeper. A foreboding ate at me, worsened by the sight of the two police cars lined up by the curb. The trouble could only be because of Tom. Well, and me. I should never have left him alone most of the day.

The greasy burger and fries I'd stopped to eat on the way home were trying to slide back up my throat as I parked. Yeah, my mother was right again. Good girls always eat right. Sure, I'd betcha a dollar to donuts, she'd meant it in a watch-your-figure kind of way instead of a you're-less-likely-to-toss your-cookies-later kind of way. Still, I do believe at some point, I needed to have a very long chat with her. Admit I now understood she had more worldly wisdom than I'd ever given her credit for. Don't ask me why I wanted to go out into the great wide world where husbands are crazy and homeless guys are wise sages. Let opposite day rule. Life back at my parents' house had been so much easier.

"Amy?!" The loud knock on my car window made me almost jump through the roof.

Peeling my gaze off the police cars, my eyes did a slow roll toward the speaker. Perfect, my landlord had dropped by. He never came to the building, ever. No, he made us poor, lowly tenants come to him.

"Amy? Lower your window so I don't have to yell!" he screamed at me again with another harsh rap on the glass.

As I tried to compose myself, I eased the crank down one careful turn at a time. Ever so grateful I drove an older than dirt car in which nothing is automatic. It'd been all I'd been able to afford when I'd left my hometown. Didn't make much at that little coffee shop, don't ya know.

What do I tell him about Tom? How do I explain the damage? Did they arrest Tom? What's the best way to protect my husband at this moment? Lord, if I've ever needed Your help, I need it now!

"Yes, Mr. Vance?" My sweetest voice, bubbly, joyful. Sugar makes everything better. One hand attached to the gearshift, the other creeping toward the keys.

Start the car, girl. Make a break for it! Yeah, my inner voice was rather conflicted at that instant.

"Your apartment's been vandalized. The police have been trying to find you, but you called in sick to work. So, they summoned me. From court no less." His fingers began to tap on the roof of my car, creating this weird echo. "The officers need you to do a walk-through with them to make sure nothing was stolen. I was unable to help since I do not keep an inventory of what my tenants do or do not own. Do you understand?" He barked at me as he leaned in my window, his hot breath on my cheek.

Was that a hint of garlic? Didn't he say he'd been in court? Never mind.

We were almost nose to nose – so uncomfortable. He eyed me like he had a witness on the stand. Well, I guess that's what that must feel like. I've never been in court. But people say in addition to being a very strict landlord, Mr. Vance was a very tough attorney. He stood about six and a half feet tall, super skinny type. His form so straight that I was certain they coined the phrase "bean pole" for him. He always dressed in designer suits, silk ties, and oxfords. Okay, there were only a few opportunities where I had the unfortunate pleasure to meet with him. Plus, he had a hankie in the suit pocket to match his tie. His black hair trimmed high and tight. Never once did I see him smile or frown or make any facial expression for that matter.

When I'd gone to his law office to apply for the apartment, he grilled me for about half an hour. For the most part, he asked about things I never thought someone should ask a prospective tenant about. Like, how many boyfriends had I had. Would I bring dates to the apartment? Did I like to party? Well, those were easy questions to answer at the time. None, never, no way, no how. Fortunate thing for me he never asked about marital status. He made the assumption I hadn't walked down the aisle already. Shame on him.

Getting back to the current issue, I replied a little too quick, "Yes, sir," to his statement of the moment. Since his head remained in my window, I slid out the passenger side. Ended up catching my thigh on the gearshift in the process, sending pain shooting down my leg. Serves me right, I was returning Mr. Vance's stare rather than looking at what I was doing. Still and all, it seemed easier than continuing to wilt under his glare. In a minute, I'd confess to every crime in the book no doubt about it.

Trying to walk with as much confidence as I could, I marched up the few steps to my door with my head held as high as possible. Mr. Vance's eyes drilled holes into my back as I as did so. His keen intellect told him something was up. Or maybe my guilt had started to eat me alive and I imagined the sensation.

Yet, I didn't have the courage to turn around to check if he was still there or not. Voices wafted from my apartment; I began to sweat. Didn't matter how cold it was out here on the landing. Still, I hesitated and mopped my dripping face. Tapping my feet, I slid in a little shuffle before deciding to go face the music.

Standing outside my door, "I'm Amy, uh..." I started to say before realizing I had another massive problem. Which last name to use? I still used my maiden's name but I shouldn't be doing so.

I had a new name but I'd never given that even once. Was that a crime? To rent an apartment under a false name? Oh brother. I hadn't gone to the driver's license place to give them an update. Yup, I could answer that one. I'd committed some act of wrongdoing because a woman had to go by her husband's name. Didn't she? Giving a shudder, I brushed these thoughts out of my head as fast as they had come.

Rushing on and hoping the officers hadn't noticed I hadn't given my full name, I added, "This is my place. I live here. Well, sort of, I spend a lot of time at school and work. So, well, really, I come here to sleep for the most part. Oh, and sometimes I grab a bite to eat here. And well..." My pent-up breath came out with a whoosh. Oh, goodness, now I'd started babbling like some lunatic.

"Well not anymore, ma'am." A deep male voice called from somewhere far inside the room.

Uh oh, had Tom done a lot more damage after I'd left? Well, duh, of course he had. Look at how much chaos he'd created when he'd broken in while I slept! "It can't be all that bad, can it?" I replied in my best singsong-y voice.

You know that happy, chirpy voice of people who can spit in the face of the devil and still come out smelling like a rose? Not like I could claim to be one of those people anymore. No, my luck had taken a serious turn for the worse today. Okay, things had gone south before now but I'd ignored the problems until right at that moment. Well, at least I pretend things were all well and good as I went about my life – a life, which for the most part, I'd dreamed up.

Tall, dark, and dreamy walked out of my apartment door. My jaw hit the floor. Where was he six months ago? Because this was grade-A beef, not chopped liver like what I had settled for. Oh, wait, that's right. Of course, it was rather obvious where he'd been and why he hadn't been an option on the menu. He'd been right here in the "city" the whole time. While I was in my tiny hometown, buried under a mountain of rules the church and my parents heaped upon me. Our stars weren't rotating in the same orbit. Shoot. Moving on.

His bright blue eyes contrasted with his dark brown hair and tanned skin. His tight blue jeans hugged his curves. A dark maroon shirt and black blazer finished the look. And these killer black cowboy boots were on his feet. Must be a detective, not the best sign for my poor husband. No, I wasn't thinking in terms of me having an affair with the man. Despite how much of a visceral reaction my body had to the guy, this wasn't where my mind went. My thoughts ran down paths of how much trouble Tom must be in. You know, as in a long prison term versus a few hours of community service. Detectives spelled trouble with a capital T. At least that was true in all the cop shows. Detectives didn't get called in for the minor stuff. Fender bender? Call a beat cop. Kill somebody? Call a detective.

"Ma'am, whoever broke in here is the worst graffiti artist I've ever seen. Unfortunately, that's only the tip of the iceberg when it comes to the damage. There was a fire in the kitchen and nothing in there is salvageable. The bathroom's a wreck. Most of your furniture's damaged. We need to do a walk-through to see what's missing. You up to doing that?" He put a hand on my shoulder, trying to comfort me in the face of adversity. I wanted to melt under the weight of it, for more than a few reasons.

"Yes, sir," I croaked out which took everything in me to do.

Fine, I'll be the first to admit I should've told the truth right then. I was very aware of what was going on. The name of the culprit lay on the tip of my tongue. I'd let the low-down scoundrel into my home, okay, not exactly. He'd broken into my apartment. But for pity sakes, I had married the guy. But nooo... I slunk into my apartment like a criminal trying to pull one over on this hunk of a cop.

Now how did women worm out of tickets in the movies? Thrust out their chests, sashay a little bit, flip their hair. Come on, you can do this, Amy! This is the best way to protect Tom! He needs counseling not prison!

The first look from the doorway took every ounce of air from me as my whole body froze in a tense cramp. Forget trying to use my feminine wiles; we weren't getting out of this mess. Tom's shiny artwork covered every wall. My few pieces of furniture had been shoved into a huge pile in the far corner. Even so, they still hadn't escaped the wrath of the condiments or whatever had been used as paint. My migraine started to come back with a vengeance, the drummer in my head banging out his best heavy metal tune. I sensed I was moments away from passing out. The dizziness coming in waves began to make the whole room sway into a weird psychedelic pattern.

We crept along, neglecting the kitchen. Indeed, the kitchen resembled a bombed-out shell when it came into view. The walls blackened, and the stove was missing. The artwork from earlier had melted into brown streaks running down the walls. About then, I realized that the place reeked of smoke. Yes, it had smelled that way when I'd left hours ago, so I guess it seemed normal now somehow.

Next came the bathroom and more "artwork." From the different texture and style, I'd have to say it was done with all my make-up this time. Huh, this piece I almost liked. So much softer, almost looked like wildflowers in a meadow, grass waving in the wind. My tension eased for a moment as I mulled over the swirls and whirls of the mural reflecting in the mirror. Nice, very nice. If Tom did something like this on a canvas, maybe I'd be able to sell a piece or two. We'd have some money for a change. Or maybe the insanity of the scene had started to infect me a little bit too much.

Moving on, we finished the tour of the disaster zone in my bedroom. My bras were strung on a line across the length of the room but nothing else was touched as far as I could tell. They looked like a pretty rainbow, lighter colors on one end all the way to the black one at the other end.

Without thinking, I reached into the top right drawer of my dresser, my body on autopilot. I snagged one of my emergency chocolate bars from my stash. Staring at my bras, I began to peel the wrapper off the treat and took a tiny nibble. Then another. Then another. Why the bras? Why not the panties too? Darn, I'd finished the chocolate. I grabbed one more. Started to eat it too.

This felt like a kill yourself with candy and sugar kind of a day. Maybe I needed to find an adult who could buy me some wine to go with it.

What wine goes with chocolate at a condiment art and lingerie viewing? Or should I just ask for something that pairs with modern art? Or skip the wine altogether and go for the tequila shots? Hum, so many choices...

"Ma'am?" A husky voice broke into my thoughts and musing. The voice of officer... *Oh, did he have a name? Other than, "Darn, he's fine!"* Heavens to Betsy, I shouldn't have been thinking that while standing here gawking at my bras. Why did I have so much fun shopping after I'd left my parents and got a job? Honest, I worked my tail off for underwear? Should've used that money for more important things instead. Like paying for heat. And food. And a better place to live. And a car that wasn't a windup toy. Oh, and I guess I needed to add a psychiatrist for my husband to the list. Because this was so beyond anything I thought anyone could be capable of doing.

Turning, I tried to gaze at only the detective's eyes. "Um, er, oh, yeah, sorry. What did you say your name was again?"

Those deep pools of blue were so wonderful! I just wanted to... snap out of it! You're a married woman and can't have these thoughts! You must be pure, a woman of virtue at all times. Oh, never mind, that ship's already sailed. Don't forget, the thoughts are as bad as the act. I sucked in my cheeks, almost swallowing my tongue in the process. Gagging, I wiggled around my head to gain some control over myself.

"Detective Martin O'Hara, ma'am. I understand this is all a bit overwhelming and traumatic. Your home was violated. But right now, I do need you to do a more thorough examination of your property to ascertain if anything is missing." He stated all of that in a commanding, firm voice. His strong arms crossed on his barrel of a chest. His legs were spread far apart as he looked down on me like I was a wayward child called to the principal's office. Well, he was doing his best to kill a girl's mood. Which was a blessing, I must say.

"Yes, sir." I walked over to my nightstand, tempted to give him a salute before I did. Opening the top drawer with a quick yank, I found my few items of jewelry had remained untouched, no tampering here. My grandmother's pearls, my aunt's earrings, my mother's rings.

Oh, no, shoot. My wedding ring sat there winking up at me. Had the officer looked in there? And if he had, did he understand the significance of this ring in particular? Right, I get it. Where was that ring supposed to be? Shining on my finger, not stuffed in the bottom of a drawer. But before I'd ever made the move here, I'd taken it off one night to wash dishes. And then forgot to put it back on. Well, that's what I always told myself – a little lie to justify my actions. I didn't want a reminder of Tom branded on me. Thus, the ring had come along for the ride with my other jewelry which I seldom wore either.

All of my jewelry not much more than junk, costume pieces, no real gold or diamonds among the bunch. Still, that band of silver placed on my hand by my husband should've meant something to me. Yet, I couldn't remember the last time I'd looked at it, much less worn it. Shame on me.

But today, Ike had reminded me that marriage wasn't something you could slip on and off. This ring stood as a symbol of the commitment I'd made. I started to place it on my finger, but knowing it would look odd if I did, I stopped myself. Later, when I was alone and not facing this inquisition would be a much better time. I'd come home to help my husband, and it was still my intention to do just that.

I didn't care about anything else in the apartment, well, not much. "The only thing of value is my jewelry which is still here, safe and sound." I clicked my fingers on the dresser, wondering why I cared about these things. My husband was the important point here. I should be asking for some help for him. However, this policeman wasn't here to give that type of assistance.

"What about your furniture?" he responded from somewhere behind me. I wasn't about to turn and have another peep at him. No, if I did that, I'd fall into his arms and beg him to run away with me. Take me away from the nightmare that is now my life. My world where it's normal to talk to homeless bums, where smoke-filled apartments were ordinary, and I'm now contemplating getting drunk. And where husbands weren't to be trusted for a second.

"Oh, the painting on those pieces is going to be an improvement. Trust me on that. If not, that's okay as well, since I got all the furniture out of the dumpsters or from the free bin or at the thrift store. Everything is a lot more expensive here than I thought it would be. Plus, college is taking up more time than I thought it would, so I only work part-time. So, I'll just scrounge around for more things if I don't like how they look now." I swiveled to face him again, my stomach cramping with the quick movement. "Can I go?"

"Please take any personal items with you that you can't live without for a while. Mr. Vance will have to find someplace for you to stay." He gave me a funny look, his head cocked to one side, his eyebrows drawn down.

"Yes, sir," I replied.

Reaching into my closet, I grabbed my two battered suitcases. Everything I owned fit into them. Well, not the furniture or kitchen stuff. No big deal. My idea of living in my car looked like an ideal plan once again. I could protect such a small space from the chaos that was Tom. Or at least I hoped so. Because of the way my parents raised me, I could live on snack food, cook on a campfire at the lake sometimes, and sleep almost anywhere. I could make this work. No, this would work with no problems at all. Save me a lot of money, hassle, and aggravation. Maybe fewer migraines too.

Yes, car perfection – apartment chaos. How much damage could Tom do in such a confined space like a car? Not much. His truck appeared to be rather unscathed all things considered. It'd be like we each had our own home, living side by side in our respective spaces. He could come and go as he pleased.

As I started to pack, Detective O'Hara sat on my bed, crossed his legs, and cleared his throat. So far, he hadn't asked me a single question about what had happened in my home, but I sensed him winding up for that now.

"So, any thoughts as to what went down here?" His query seemed more like an accusation, and it hit me like a brick.

When the pain of the first volley had eased a tad, my fingers played with my lips, muffling my reply, "Uhm, not really." No, no thoughts. I wasn't going to think about anything other than getting my bras out of the view of this man as fast as possible. I always stayed alone in my little bubble I'd created and for excellent reasons. Until now, that is, when this gorgeous hunk of a guy sat there watching me play with all of my underthings like it wasn't any big deal. Biting my lip, I pressed on with my task, stuffing down my humiliation and the bile rising up my throat.

"No guys from school who've asked you out and you rebuffed?" He examined my every move, his eyes darting back and forth with each step I took.

Such an easy answer. "No." For once, being a hermit had a plus side. Having no real friends of any kind – male or female – had been rather lonely at times. Nevertheless, right at this moment, straining under the microscope of the detective, my odd habits were paying off. And I got to tell the truth to that inquiry.

Yes, last bra down and out of sight.

On to my dresser drawers now. Not much in there. This would be quick.

How do I get my panties out without him seeing them too? Ugh, he's going to see that all my bras have a pretty panty to match!

"Any guy following you around? Work, school, here?" This question also asked as he stared at me, with me doing my best to not do anything more than peep at him from time to time.

"No." I swallowed hard.

Now, come on, Mr. Hot Shot Detective, you're throwing me nothing but softballs. The problem isn't following me. He's married to me. No, don't think about Tom! You'll end up blurting something you shouldn't.

Grabbing all my panties in a huge bunch, I threw them into a suitcase. The burning in my gut told me this little question and answer session wasn't going as well as I imagined it was.

"So, what was the deal with the male clothing on the landing this morning?" His inquiries were coming in rapid-fire succession now. His voice seemed to be getting deeper as he went along. And he appeared to be getting sexier by the minute, thus I didn't glance at him at all.

"Not really sure. I don't have any clothing for a man here." It could've been anyone's, and I'm not a crossdresser. Moving onto the drawer which contained my t-shirts and shorts, I also tossed them carelessly into the case.

See, Mr. Detective, my t-shirts are lacy and all girl. My mother made sure the older I got the less I dressed like a boy. Nothing for you to worry about now.

"Were you the one who removed the smoke detectors?" This he asked in an almost gruff growl; his voice had lowered so much.

"No." Again, simple was my plan as my fingers squeezed a shirt into a ball. Onto my closet and my dresses and jeans. Folding a luxury I didn't have time for. I could always iron things again later. Grab and stuff were my sole goals at that point. Anything to escape this man before things went even further south.

"Your neighbors reported a scruffy homeless guy about your age in the area this morning. Brown hair, slouched over, baggy clothing. Know him?" His voice seemed to soften. Was he wanting to win me over to his side? If so, it wasn't going to work.

"Um, not that I can say." I nibbled on my fingernail.

See, you can tell the officer the truth without telling him a single useful bit of information! You don't know anything about Tom, and you never will. This whole thing with the apartment has proved that. Because, how can you solve the puzzle of a person who thinks there are spies who listen to your conversations? Or is so high he destroys things? Nope, beyond me.

Last thing. I shoved my jewelry case into my purse. "All done." Seizing a suitcase in each hand, I turned and took a direct look at him again. One long, lingering gaze from the toes of his beautiful polished boots to the crown of his lush locks. And I gulped down my drool before it started running down my chin.

Yet, when he smiled and showed perfect white teeth, my longing for this man came to a screeching halt. No, I wasn't smitten with that grin the way I'd been with Ike's. Go figure that one. He rose with a slow grace like a dancer would do.

"Here, let me take those," he whispered. Our hands touched for a moment as he grasped the handles. To my surprise, the spark between us lit in an unmistakable way as a tingle wound up my arms. I'd never come close to this sensation with Tom. I never could have it with Tom. However, here it was with a complete stranger who wasn't here as my friend. Who, if he ever found out I lied to him, would arrest me faster than Tom could disappear. Which, in this case, wasn't fast enough based on the damage I'd seen.

And that is why I could never leave my husband alone ever again. The man was a danger to himself and others. Thank my lucky stars the fire hadn't spread beyond the confines of the small space I'd rented. No way did I want it on my conscience if any harm had come to the Diaz family. And I just didn't see how it would be possible to go from this disaster to finding Tom counseling so he'd be "normal." Course, I'd settle for Tom not ever doing something like this again.

"Thank you." Snatching my hands back jolted me into the real world again with a thump. Because let's face it, nothing was going to happen between us. Not in a million years. Yup, I'm too much of a good girl. While the affair option sounded pretty great right about then, it wasn't a road to take. For the simple reason, it would be beyond stupid given the predicament I was in. Yeah, the problem with Tom wasn't something I could solve by landing in an even bigger mess.

Out in the parking lot, Martin – er, um, Detective O'Hara put my suitcases in the backseat of my car. Mr. Vance had left and you bet I felt gratitude for that. I spotted a note slipped under my wiper blade, letting me know which hotel he'd booked me into. While I didn't glimpse at the page, I was sure it would be the cheapest place in town and more of a dump than my apartment.

"We'll be in touch. But you can call me if you think of anything useful," the wonderful detective said with a grand wave as he turned to head back to the place I'd once called my home. Didn't think it would be a safe space ever again. Didn't matter how well the remodel went.

What "we?" Oh, that's right, I heard other voices.

There were two other people in my apartment. Yet the presence of them had registered at the very edge of my consciousness. They were about as important to me as who ran for office in East Overshoe.

Chapter 12

"Ya gotta be joshin'!" Hank laughed so hard I worried he might break the window he worked at putting molding around. "Ya husband burnt ya place down? Good night. An' you'se worried 'bout a cop seein' ya undies?!" Now bent over double, he leaned his head heavy on the pane of glass, holding his sides in pain.

Yup, he was like everyone else in my life. Not seeing things from my side. As the song goes, "I been in the right place, but it must have been the wrong time. I'd have said the right thing, but must have used the wrong line." My whole life had been lived sideways and upside down. No biggie. But this should be common to me by now. People putting me down. Telling me how foolish I am. I'd had a lifetime of that. Yet for the first time ever, now was my time to stand up for myself. To have what I wanted for a change. To be my own best hero. To stop trying to fix everyone and everything else in the world. And most important, to find a way to use my truth to get my son to come back.

"Hey, enough of the teasing, okay? You're the one who said you wanted me to finish the story. So, you can't make fun of me anymore. You understand?" Huffing, I stormed off into the next room.

This room I pictured would be my cozy master suite one day. Already I could see the color of the paint on the walls – fine, there were no actual walls as of yet. Sheetrock still lay in a pile in the other room, waiting for me to hang it.

Right at that moment, only I could see this whole concept of what might be. Of the disaster house ever being livable again, ever being pretty. Before making this space my own, the opossum in the corner would have to move on. I kept kicking him out, but he always found his way back in somehow. Oh, and the bats. Please, don't forget about the mice. Ugh, I needed to stop thinking about this now, because my skin had begun to crawl at the thought of how many critters I lived with at the moment. Funny, I'd wanted nothing more than to be alone most of the time. Yet here I lived with a whole of host of roommates of the worst possible kind.

But as I rolled my shoulders to release my tension, my eyes took in everything around me. And it amazed me how much work I'd managed to do. The work had gone so quick. Yeah, yeah, all Hank and I had accomplished in such a short time. Why, oh why, couldn't the rest of my life be this simple to fix? But this wreck of a house, ah, that was easy. A quick sweep of a broom here, a bit of sheetrock there, and voila, everything would be better in no time flat.

And here I was acting like a two-year-old, off having a snit and a pout in her room. After having run away from all my problems forever, all I did was create more. By dragging my old life into my new one. Yikes. However, given the final straw situation when I'd thrown in the towel, I felt more than justified in my response. Enough had been enough. But why had I told my story to anyone? Should've left my old life in the past where it belonged and gotten my new beginning as I'd wanted. But I didn't want to leave my son back there with all of the other flotsam and jetsam. Even if he felt he didn't need or want me in his life, I knew better. A child needs his momma no matter how old and mature he thinks he is.

After a heartbeat or two, I calmed down and joined Hank back in the center part of the house. Without a word, I returned to my task for the day. We continued to work in silence for a long time. Him pounding at the nails, me cutting boards. Old-school remodeling without modern tools since there wasn't any power. Left me wondering, yet again, if I shouldn't buy a generator and a few power tools. But I still didn't see the need to speed this process up at all.

"Lady, I won't laugh no more." He placed his hand on my shoulder for a brief second as he walked by to find more molding. Nothing more than a light swipe, but still, the warmth of human connection was there.

"Thanks." I grimaced, my gut still in knots. My head screamed at me to button my lips. Yeah, I wasn't ready to start sharing again. Nope, I recognized I should've lied from the instant I'd met Hank. Said something along the lines of I wanted to live somewhere it didn't snow. Nothing more, nothing less. You know – KISS. Keep it simple, stupid. That would've been so much better, because this wasn't getting me even an inch closer to Paul.

The next day, I made the decision it was beyond time to turn the tables on Hank.

"Hey, while I do appreciate you being here every day, why aren't you in school? You told me you were done, but you can't be old enough for that." I looked him square in the eye. If he wanted to work all day like an adult, then he needed to answer a few questions.

"Ah, yeah. Ended up in a mess. Ma sent me to my granddaddy. But I say school is out. He say, no trouble. But I gots to earn some dough. Pull my weight." He stared at me with more than a touch of ice in his eyes, his hands curled into tight balls.

"Cool?" He barked out this as a question, yet, to me, it seemed he didn't want an answer.

I could take it or leave it, but this was how things were.

"Is your mother here?" I asked as I pushed some more insulation and steel wool into a crack. Anything to keep the critters from coming in, though so far nothing had worked. My little friends returned each and every evening to keep me company.

"She was. But she ain't now. She got a new friend an' left." He shrugged as his back came up to full height, his chest out, his chin raised in the air.

Ah, I thought I'd gotten the picture here and wasn't going to press for more. His mother wasn't the greatest single parent on the planet, and he'd acted out because of it. Thank heavens his grandfather had stepped in and did appear to be making the kid fly straight. Or at least straighter. Working was better than hanging out with the wrong crowd.

But it hurt my soul to think this boy didn't have the love of a mother. I wanted to wrap my arms around him and never let him go. He acted too much like a man and not enough like a boy. He should be enjoying his last few years of innocence. Still, I was more than aware it wasn't my place to say anything about his upbringing. All I could do was ensure he continued to do an adequate job for me and provide a reference when we finished.

And his work ethic was beyond reproach. He showed up, did whatever I asked without complaint, and do so with an eye to detail. Whoever he'd worked with before had taught him well. Every time I examined Hank's achievements; my heart swelled with pride. I'm sure I paid more than the going rate for a teenage helper, not that I minded. He felt more like a partner than anything else and I had the funds to provide for his needs and wants. Didn't matter to me what the situation at his home might be.

As the work progressed, the days dragged on. Although the calendar stated the season to be fall, the heat and humidity weren't letting up in the least. My constant state of being was damp – wrung out and hung up to dry in a sauna. I began to think mushrooms were growing on my toes. Something green grew on my shoes and suitcases. One thing I would never need to own again in my life was a humidifier.

Plus, I came to believe the gas station around the corner began to think I wanted to work there. After all, I traipsed in there at all hours of the day and night – to use the restroom, of course, not to buy anything. Oh, no, I'd waltz in there, do my business, and walk back out without saying a word to anyone. I didn't have any desire to explain to anyone why I didn't live in a home with a working toilet. Forget working. I hadn't ordered one as yet. Just one more thing on a very long and ever-growing list.

The solar shower I'd brought with me worked out alright for quick wash-ups. Lucky, or unlucky, for me, it rained every other day and I collected plenty of water for its use. Thank goodness for my popup rain barrel which had also been in my overstuffed, well-stocked suitcases. In addition, I used the extra water for washing my dishes after I cooked. Ah, the basic lifestyle of camping. But I do believe it rained more here in a week than in a year back in my home state. Did make things a might more difficult when one tried to survive the roughing-it life. Dampness crept into everything.

Plenty of sunshine in the mornings kept my mini solar charger working. Thus, my phone and tablet never died on me. Living in the woods for so long had taught me so many little tricks. I knew how to survive on nothing and could keep this up for years if I had to. However, I didn't believe the project required that much time given the pace we were making on the house.

Yup, things were working out fine as far as I could tell. To be fair, others didn't see it the same and that was clear as day. I now looked rather rough around the edges, not the lady I'd been for years. My t-shirts and shorts became stained and had holes from the remodel. My hair grew out, and the humidity in the area made it frizzy. Thus, I'd started pulling it into a loose ponytail most days. I wore these cheap tennis shoes I'd found at a dollar store I'd discovered when I'd wandered around the neighborhood one day. No socks, just the shoes to keep a tad bit cooler. After about the fifth day of wearing the stupid things, my big toes popped out of each of them. Not like I cared in the least. I'd reverted back to the tomboy of my youth, and it was the best thing ever.

A nice policeman took to stopping by almost every day. He gave the impression he didn't agree with my lifestyle. At first, he'd sit in his patrol car across the street and watch what I was up to. I'd tried to get a proper look at him, without being too obvious about it. But all I could tell was that he was dark, his skin blending into the color of his uniform.

Later, he'd drive behind me when I'd walked to the gas station. He'd drive around the block when Hank left each evening. Then one afternoon, as I worked on the porch alone, he got out of his car and ambled over. Standing in my yard, he planted himself like a sturdy tree as he looked up and down at the house, then at me as well. Oh, crud, the man before me was none other than that Jessie guy from the coffee shop.

I returned his gaze. "Can I help you?" I didn't want to be rude to the man, but for the life of me, I couldn't figure out why he'd been watching me for so long. As in days and weeks, gosh, I wasn't sure at this point. Was this his idea of getting to know someone? Watching their every move?

"Do you have a permit to occupy?" He didn't move any closer. His hands crossed into a ball at his midsection, his head tilted this way and that.

"Uhm, since I don't have a clue what that is, I'd have to say no." I gulped, my tongue almost sticking to the roof of my mouth. I had a permit to do the renovations. I'd gotten that online before I'd ever set foot in town. The website hadn't mentioned this other thing.

"Well, since this premise remained unoccupied for so long you needed one before you started living here." He moved to put his hands on his hips, his legs out wide. His finger tapped on the butt of his gun. Was he wanting a good ol' fashioned shootout at high noon? All I had was a caulk gun, buried somewhere inside the house in a mound of tools.

"Okay, I'll look into that. Thank you for filling me in. Anything else?" I rubbed my hand across the rail I'd been installing, the wood soft as butter. I'd carved a rounded detail into it earlier and looked forward to picking the stain color later.

"Sleep somewhere else until you get it." He spun on his heels and marched back to his waiting car. No fuss, no muss.

Seemed Jessie the coffee guy was very different from Jessie Mr. Policeman. Watching his retreating back, a temptation bubbled up to say something snarky in reply. Yet, I knew it would get me nowhere. In the end, it wouldn't matter anyway, I could sleep in the backyard just as well as in the unfinished house. Both had about the same amount of creature comforts. Since my air mattress was portable, moving it wasn't a big deal. Well, come to think of it, the yard was better in at least one respect. All the animals in the area lived in the house. I'd have the yard all to myself.

A few days later, Jessie got out of his car again. Quick steps took him to my side yard where I'd begun to sand the wall, prepping it for priming at some future date. "Hello again, sir." I leaned down a little to get a better view of him from the ladder. "What can I do you for today?" I was half tempted to call him by his first name. But since he didn't appear to want this level of familiarity while on the job, I refrained.

"When I said you couldn't live here, I meant on the property," he huffed, his hand tapping out a rhythm on his leg.

"Oh, okay. I guess I don't understand the problem. Homeless people sleep on the street. So why exactly can't I sleep on my grass?" I began to crawl down the ladder so I'd be at his level.

"Because it's not safe." He reached up his hand to take mine. Then using his other hand to grab my waist, he swung me to the ground with the grace of a ballerina. I wasn't wearing a skirt, so I didn't float on air. No, instead he'd found me in the state of being a sloppy, stinky mess from head to toe. Paint chips and dust stuck to every inch of me.

"This is the safest I've been in years." Giving him a shrug, my hands waved in the air. Oh my, this man had never stared at a bear and walked away. Or met my former husband.

He started to choke. "Look. I don't know where you're from, but…" He waggled a narrow finger in my face. "I can get you fixed up with a good mental health person."

"Oh, no need. I'm not crazy, not by a long shot. Don't worry. I'll get this little matter resolved." I chuckled as I patted his strong arm. "Nothing to worry about. Anything else?"

"Guess not." He shoved my hand away. "I just can't seem to figure you out."

"Well, you certainly were trying to the other day at the coffee shop." My nose wiggled, I so needed to sneeze right about then.

"Uhm, well." He spun and began marching back to the street. "I'll see you around, you need lots of help, ma'am."

After he left, with more than a few backward glances as he went, I made a few phone calls. And two hours later, a small five-foot by five-foot shed arrived. Easy peasy. After cutting a hole in the back and making a fake window, I was set for life. Come to think of it, the stupid shed might've been one of the nicest places I'd ever lived.

All the while, Hank kept pestering me to go on about my husband Tom. He asked if I was still married, what had happened after the fire, and so on. I diverted the subject every time.

One morning, Hank showed up with a wicked shiner. "What happened, honey?" I stopped my task of the morning, putting my paintbrush down in the tray.

"Dude say my mama's a whore." Hank put his fingers up to his swollen face, gingerly pushing around the worst of the dark marks. "I got all up in his grill."

"Do you want me to go grab some ice?" I gulped. I wanted to treat him like a man, but I also didn't want him going around getting in fights.

"Naw. I good. Dude look worse than me!" He chuckled. "Ya gonna tell my granddaddy?" He gave me a sheepish grin. He sensed what he'd done was wrong.

"Hank, I don't see how you are going to be able to hide that face from him." I patted his shoulder.

"Yea. I knows." He hung his head for a moment. "But I can try, like ya hid stuff ya husband did?" He gave me a sly little smile.

Oh no. Was I giving this kid the wrong impression here? That it was fine and dandy for adults to not be honest? "That was wrong of me to have done. Please, don't do as I did back then. I've learned my lesson. Trust me on that." I leaned against the wall, giving out a sigh. If I'd told my son something, maybe I'd still be part of his life.

"Oh." He turned and started to prep himself for the task of the day.

After a moment or two of watching him, I returned to my painting. We worked in silence for a while. He cut away at some boards, and I turned the world blue.

"I knows why ya mad about me laughin' at ya. It same as me with the dude, yeah?" He dropped the saw; the metal twanged as it hit the floor.

"Yes, honey. That's exactly it. He hurt your feelings; you hurt mine. Only, lucky for you, I don't beat people up over it." I chuckled for a second. "It's a matter of respect."

"Got ya." He nodded several times before bending over to pick up the tool. "I don't do it no mo'."

I went back to my job, thinking about all of it. My heart told me to keep talking. This was the best way to practice what to say to Paul. Because if I got everything straight in my head, I'd be able to speak the next time. Unlike the first time when I'd caved quicker than a house of cards sat on by a toddler. These memories had been stuffed down for so long, forgotten because I didn't want to deal with them. But if I ever wanted a chance to make things right with my son, I'd have to face them at some point. Oh, and find a way to get my son to agree to meet me somewhere or at least talk on the phone. Well, here went nothing.

"Okay, Hank, today I'm going to tell you the next piece. But I swear if you give me one little chortle or snort, not only am I going to stop the story, but I'm going to fire you." I waved a paintbrush his way, leaving a few drops of bright blue paint splattered on the already dirty and stained floor. In case anyone wondered – the new flooring would be the last thing done. Easier that way, no drop cloths required while painting.

"Ya betcha, lady. No probs here!" He gave me a goofy grin, way too much like Ike's for my liking.

"Umm, where was I now…" I tapped my finger against my cheek, squinting my eyes.

"Ya was leavin' you'se place after the fire," Hank volunteered.

"Ah, yes. That's right." I dipped the brush back in the paint, hesitating a moment before putting it back on the wall. I'd left my wall paintings and photos behind. I'd need artwork at some point, from a professional this time. Not things I'd created. "Well, I knew at that point what I needed most was to find Tom…."

Chapter 13

My stomach churned as I drove away from the parking lot for the second time in one day. Each bump made the bile rise in my throat and my head pulse with white-hot pain. I had to find my husband before the police did. It was as simple as that. However, who in the world would have any clue where Tom might be? Yeah, yeah, I get it. I should've had some idea; he was my husband after all.

Pulling into the same convenience store from earlier in the morning, a bad case of déjà vu hit me. You know like that movie *Groundhog Day*? This day was never going to end. I was going in circles, destined to do the same things over and over again. Perhaps I should go back to the beach at the lake and find Ike. He'd been a lovely distraction the first time he'd shown up like a genie from a lamp.

Beating my fingers on the steering wheel, I tried to think of who to call. My mother of course. She's who I should've called first thing in the morning before I ever dared to face Tom. One word from me and she'd drop everything, rush right up here. Even if she'd always sworn she'd never leave her hometown anymore. She would've for me. And she'd have arrived about the time the fire happened from the looks of things. No way could I have explained that whole fiasco. Or where might be Tom right now. And about then, she'd start asking questions I couldn't answer. Forget it. I'm not speaking to my mother. Not now. Maybe not ever again.

Again, I had no idea how much about Tom my father knew. Or how much he'd shared with my mother. And I wanted to protect them from finding out any more than they absolutely had to. Tom was my problem, not theirs. My father picked Tom for a reason, and I couldn't go running home for each little thing that popped up. My parents never had gone to visit my grandparents after all. They handled all their difficulties all by themselves.

Reaching into the glove box, I pulled out migraine pill number two for the day.

When was the last time you've had a day where you've need two doses?

Never. Let me repeat that. Never, ever. My doctor would have a fit when I called in for a refill so soon. Speaking of such, it was almost time for my annual physical. Had I remembered to make the appointment? No, because I didn't want to go back to my hometown. I needed to find a new doctor here and hope they'd be willing to squeeze me in soon. Because sometimes offices can take forever to give you an appointment.

Oh, my word, Amy. Focus! You are so off on a rabbit trail....

Twiddling my fingers, I got down to the matter at hand. Let me see. Tom can't have a job somewhere out there in the great big world. His assertion that he had must've been a lie from the beginning. The whole "I travel for my job" line nothing more than a flat-out con. Who'd hire someone who leaned toward the nutty side and disappeared for months on end? No one.

Moving on. Does he have friends? No way. For the same reason as he was unemployed. Hmm, now who does that leave? He was new in our little town; I remember my father mentioning that. I also remember something about the church.

My pastor from home! That's who I should call. Tom must've visited the church at some point... the men's group, yup. Not sure if that was how things happened, but it made some sense.

And there it was, something to go on. A thin little thread to pull which might lead to something. So off to the payphone I went.

"Hello?" a male voice answered after several rings. So many in fact, I'd almost given up and hung up the receiver.

"Hi, Pastor Sanderson. It's Amy." I wrinkled my nose and pressed my lips together. I hadn't gone home for Christmas break and broke my mother's heart. My pastor had been very quick to call me up and tell me so. During that phone call, my beloved pastor had wagged his finger the whole time. Okay, I couldn't see it, but boy could I sense it. The man was a master at shaming you for every little thing you did wrong.

"Oh, how are you doing, Amy?" he puffed out.

Why was he breathing so hard? Did I catch him at a bad time?

"How's everything back home?" Might as well get this over with, butter him up some before stating my case. My fingers scratched the back of my head as I leaned on the glass wall of the booth.

"Fine, child. You must come back for a least a quick visit." He sighed. "But you need something or else you wouldn't have called. How can I help?"

"Can you tell me where Tom works?" Biting my lip, I pressed on and ignored his reference to the fact I'd only call out of desperation. And the fact that I'd just admitted I'd lied when I left home. "Or his mother's number or address?"

"Umm..." His voice trailed off. "Everything alright there?"

"I'd be doing better if I found Tom." Why won't he answer my questions? Maybe I should call back later? But then again, I sounded rather silly. What wife doesn't have even an inkling of where her husband might be?

"Should I call your parents? What's wrong with your husband now?" He huffed so loud I moved the receiver away from my ear.

I clenched my teeth hard enough that the click echoed in the confined space. My jaw hurt from the effort of not screaming at my pastor. And by now I clutched the poor phone receiver so tight it surprised me I hadn't pulverized it. This conversation was getting me nowhere fast, because of course, the man knew my husband had gone missing after the wedding and I'd moved without him.

"I'm not sure if something's wrong which is why I need to find him." The walls felt like they were closing in on me.

"Well, I'm not sure how to get in touch with his mother, but I can tell you his former address. Maybe he's there. I think he had a roommate." A rustling noise came over the phone, muffling his answer. "His employer was an out-of-state firm before you got married. But I thought he got a new job when you two moved?"

Roommate? I thought he'd said he lived with his mother. Or was I the first, last, and only person Tom had shared that tidbit of info with? Oh, I remembered. When we'd first met, Tom had mentioned something about bunking with a buddy. And there was no way I was going to respond to the question. Yup, he'd picked up on my lie. I didn't want to compound my first lie about Tom's work with a second.

"Sure. Maybe his roommate will be of some help." I began to tap my foot, almost doing a little dance in the tiny phone booth.

"Here it is." He gave me an address in a small town about an hour away. At least it was closer to my college town than my hometown. Plus, the drive seemed more inviting than going to some motel. Given the not-so-terrific state of my apartment building, I could only imagine what motel Mr. Vance had booked me into. There were exactly three options in town for hotels: the luxury resort, the family inn, and the place by the highway no one was ever sure if it was open or not. The building there looked worse than the hotel in that movie *Psycho*. No doubt, the reservation would be at option number three. Kill me now rather than in the shower later. I'd appreciate it a whole ton being saved the humiliation of being discovered dead in the buff.

"Thanks." I clicked off the line before I started swearing up a blue streak at how hard this was.

I yanked some clothes out of a suitcase. Then I rushed into the convenience store to change in the dirty bathroom. I needed a shower, but a wash-up with some paper towels to remove most of the sand off my legs was the best I could do. Shaking my skirt, sand and grit flew everywhere as I folded it. Yet the bathroom didn't look any more disgusting than when I'd entered. Not like I was up to caring about something like this at this moment. Clean jeans and an almost wrinkle-free shirt. Much better.

On my way out of the store, I grabbed some necessities for on the way – you know, chocolate, iced tea, and more chocolate. Plus a few more bars of chocolate in case the first few lasted me less than ten seconds. In the end, I was glad I had the extra bars. I ate every last one of them before ten miles had passed. Yup, killing me with kindness wasn't my style but killing me with chocolate was.

Finding the address turned out to be easy, that is when I landed in the middle of nowhere at last. There were no other houses around, just miles and miles of nothing but trees, and then this house surrounded by heavy equipment. And I do mean heavy. Backhoes. Tractors. Bulldozers. Dump trucks. Cement trucks. Drilling rigs. I swear on my life, even one of those monster trucks used in mining that are several stories tall. It was beyond weird.

However, this might explain some of my husband's odd behavior. The noise of these things starting up all the time had driven him around the bend. This was no place to live for anyone, and I couldn't understand why someone would plant a house here.

Before I got out of the car, I paused to settle myself a bit. The drive should've been relaxing. Instead, each mile seemed to ramp up my anxiety level another ten notches. Ended up to the point where I had this sensation like I could fly to Pluto and back in a few seconds flat. I took a moment for a few cleansing yoga breaths – in and out, feeling my body from my toes to my head and trying to center myself. Who was I kidding? With the day I was having, even vodka and a dozen tranquilizers weren't going to calm me down. My hands shook so much my poor little Bug shook too. Okay, time to screw my courage to the sticking place. What in heavens name did that mean anyway? My mother always said that when times got hard, but I never had a clue what it meant.

Getting out of the Bug with legs that made Jell-O seem like solid concrete, I wobbled to the front door. The house rose before me, nothing more than a bungalow gone bad. Faded purple paint on the main section of the building. Roof in serious need of new shingles. A haphazard addition on the side painted an unusual shade of burnt orange. A leaning front porch in a red rust color with horrendous fuchsia chairs. The front stairs had a giant, gaping hole in each step. But since they weren't on the same sides, the steps became a gauntlet I had to scale to even make it to the front door.

How bad did I want to find Tom?

Step one, a ginger hop to the right.

Is it worth all this effort?

Step two, an unsure slide to the left.

No, I should be letting the police find Tom.

Step three, another timid bounce to the right.

But this is my job now, taking care of Tom, because I'm going to be the best wife I can be.

Step four, to the center now, cha, cha, cha.

Whatever it takes, I have to find Tom and get him the help he needs before he gets arrested.

Jumping onto the porch, I skipped steps five and six altogether. Bad move. My right foot fell through the weak boards. This left me with one leg in a hole up to my thigh and one leg trailing behind down the steps. Plus, my nose and mouth were kissing the floor with my arms splayed wide. Thank goodness I'd changed out of my skirt.

"Now who in tarnation are you and what did you do to my porch?" A voice boomed out at me from above as if it was God. I almost wet my pants.

Wriggling around some, I managed to push myself up on my elbows to gaze toward the speaker. A figure bigger than the door frame, both in width and height, cast a shadow on me. She wore an Omar-the-tentmaker muumuu special. You know those bright neon ones, with every color of the rainbow added for effect with no discernible pattern. Her long dark brown hair hung loose and had streaks of purple and pink in it.

No doubt about it, I had the right house. This woman had "I am Tom's Mother" stamped on her forehead in flashing neon to match her dress. Yes, I was very aware that I was putting the whole family in a box full of crazy. But you gotta look at what I was dealing with here. Tom was one cloned apple rather than one that'd fallen far from the tree. He and his mom looked that much alike, well apart from the size factor. Oh, and he's a guy and she's not.

"Sorry about that," I said with as much meekness as I could muster. Trying to pry myself out of the hole, I pushed harder but for all the world I felt like I was getting more stuck. "A little help would be nice." I gulped, my throat closing on me.

"I never leave the house. You're on your own, honey. Now hurry up and tell me who you are before I grab the shotgun." She growled as she pointed her hands as if to shoot me. Then she laughed and stomped her elephant-sized foot. Not the best idea, the whole porch began to shake like an earthquake had hit it.

Not leaving the house seemed like a rather obvious statement to me. I doubt she could've gotten out of the door if she tried.

"Um, I'm Amy. I'm married to Tom Smith. Do you have any idea where he is?" The words came out as nothing more than a mouse squeak, and I wasn't sure she could hear me. But by now, the sheer fear factor was motivation enough for me to start making some headway on getting my leg out. To my horror, the hole in the porch had grown to twice the size. As I started to slither on my backside away from it toward the stairs, I heard a tearing noise. Oh crud. It could only be one thing. I'd caught my jeans on a nail. I may be about to moon the world after all.

"Ah, ain't that sweet. You're the fool who's supposed to make him finally fly straight. Guess that didn't last, huh? Well, as his mother, I knew marriage was a bad idea for him. I don't know how you talked him into it, but I wish you all the luck in the world. You're going to need it, toots. Because he's your problem now. I ain't helpin' him no more. I changed the locks even after I had him give me the key back. No way I'm letting him slink home with his tail between his legs like some lost puppy. Nope, should've put him in that home when I had the chance." She laughed again as she said this, her big mouth wide open, revealing an almost toothless grin. A gaping maw, ready to swallow me if I dared to slide even an inch closer.

But wait a cotton-picking minute. *I* talked him into marriage? Not on your fat bum, lady! In fact, it was my father's bright idea that this was the perfect man for me. I'd gone along for the ride, well, sort of. Permission to live somewhere other than under my parents' thumb was all I sought. But now wasn't the time to argue with this woman. Still, I now realized why Tom didn't have any guests at the wedding. His mother was housebound, and he didn't have a friend in the world.

"Um, what *home* are you referring to?" Against my better judgment, I had to know.

"When he was first diagnosed, the doctor wanted to put him in a place with others like him so he wouldn't do no harm." She gave me a funny look as she stated this, her lips curling up into a snarl. Taping her enormous foot on the floor, she rocked the porch and me with each motion.

"Diagnosed with what?" I almost didn't want to hear the answer, because the response could only be a giant can of worms I didn't need.

Oh, my goodness, did Tom have some kind of contagious disease? Something someone should've told me about before we were married?

Was this another one of those questions you should ask a potential mate? Do you have leprosy, and will we need to move to a colony somewhere super isolated? Oh, my gosh, how many people has he been in contact with? He's been in my house! Maybe the fire was a blessing in disguise after all. Fire killed germs, right? Please, please, don't let this have spread to anyone else!

"Why, bipolar of course. Why else would he believe in so many crazy things? Did you think I raised him in a cult?" She looked at me with distinct disgust, mouth clenched tight, nose wrinkled.

Based on Mrs. Smith's appearance, a cult was a definite possibility. Not one I'd ever mention, though. Not with a gun within easy reach and that she seemed to have a hair-trigger anger-wise. I wanted to go home to my cozy little bed, crawl under the covers and ignore the world. Oh, wait – that's right. I don't have a home anymore. Tom destroyed almost everything I owned. This is why I needed to find him quickly, I didn't want him out there damaging anything else.

"No, ma'am." My instincts kicked in. As polite as could be, I showed my dimples.

By now I'd eased to the edge of the steps, and I felt the back of my jeans. Sure enough, a hole the size of the Grand Canyon was there. There was no way to leave this dwelling with any scrap of dignity in place. Today, I'd worn my lacy red bra and panty set. The panties are see-through by the way. I haven't a clue why I'd thrown them on this morning, given the situation in my apartment at the time. But there you have it, my red flag to the world that I was about to raise high and wave as proud as could be. This particular underwear set made me feel brave on an average day. Today, it matched the color my face was fast becoming. I planned on burning it when the sun set because I wasn't ever going to wear it again. Nope, I was going back to being properly dressed at all times. As my mother always used to tell me, "When you leave the house, wear your cleanest, newest pair of white underwear. You never know when you'll get in an accident, dear."

"Well, I best be going now. Thanks for your time. I'll send you some money to fix the porch." Crawling down the steps on my knees, I rose when I reached the solid ground of the grass.

Her tiny, rodent-like eyes watched me as I strolled backward to my car. I did my cute little princess wave as I climbed in the passenger side, never once turning around. Wasn't the easiest thing to pry the car door open using my hand behind my back. Yet, I managed it somehow. Two seconds before I gave a sigh of relief that no one had seen my undies, I heard a knock on the driver's window. Spinning my head, I saw a brute of a construction worker standing by my car. Hard hat, funny orange neon vest, the works.

Squirming into the proper seat, I rolled down the window as quick as possible. "Yes?" My voice dripped with sweet honey. But I knew this wasn't going to end well, not with the condition I'd left the porch. How long had he stood there beside my car? I winced at the thought, my body tensing.

"Thanks for the show. All the guys loved it." His face, all lit up like a Christmas tree, said more than his words. He hooked his thumb over his shoulder and pointed to a pickup truck a little way up the street. Five or six guys hung out the back. They all gave me similar smiles and waves. The man by my car then patted the roof so hard it sounded like I was inside a bell before he started to walk off. Almost back at the truck, he turned and gave me a deep bow from his waist.

Oh, my word. My head hit the steering wheel, as every inch of me sank with the realization of what these men had seen. Why hadn't the porch swallowed me? Or my new mother-in-law shot me? Well of course, where construction equipment is stored, there's gotta be a few construction guys. Why hadn't I thought about that? I should've slid the whole way to my car on my backside. But nooo. I strolled along like I didn't have a care in the world who saw me.

Who moons construction workers? Me. What have I become? Is this what marriage has turned me into? A stripper? A flasher? My mother was going to kill me. That is, if I ever confessed it to her. Yet there was no way in heck I was ever telling anyone about this little incident. Thank my lucky stars mama Smith was a shut-in, who was she gonna tell? No one, would be my best guess.

Chapter 14

I halted my story, my shame from that moment so long ago as fresh now as ever. Then, a different feeling washed over me as I looked back on this whole incident. Without warning, not laughing at the memory became difficult. Hindsight often views things in such a way as to soften the harsh lines. Blurring the straight and narrow into hazy swirls. How was Hank not busting a gut right now? I glanced over at him. His back faced me, his forehead on the wall. And his shoulders jiggled up and down like waves crashing onshore. I decided to put him out of his misery.

"Go ahead and laugh. I can see it's killing you not to." My stomach pulled in tight as I breathed in deep.

The fresh paint fumes filled my whole being as I inhaled, leaving me more than a little dizzy. Looking around, I spotted a weird whirling pattern I'd left on the wall. The grey of the drywall winked at me from under the thin layer of robin egg blue of the paint. More than ever, I was grateful I wasn't using a roller. I'd have ended up with the windows covered with the sticky stuff instead of the new walls. Nope, I'd spent the morning attempting to cut in the corners before attacking the main field so to speak. Hank had been working on spackling the screw heads on the other wall.

Behind me, his deep chortle started slow and built up to a wailing crescendo, echoing in the empty space. Whipping around, I watched him rocking on his heels. He pushed back and forth against the nearest wall.

"Ah, man lady, ya life's one mad coaster!" he wailed as he turned to face me, wiping tears from his eyes. "I didn't think adults did such things!" He slumped to the floor, slapping the boards with his hands.

"Don't even get me started on what adults do and don't do." My chuckle was much lighter than his. Maybe I should go into standup comedy. Though, all those years ago, I'd felt mortified at the whole event.

"So, what was ya majoring in at school? Disaster 101?" His howls of laughter once again rang out in the room.

"You would think so, but no. Religious studies. However, I never used my degree. Just stayed on at the place I worked as a secretary when I was in school."

I sighed deep as a surge of regret washed over me. That part of the story untold and should stay that way. The humiliation involved with that was so intense that it was almost worse than anything else. No church would hire me after I graduated. At the time, devastation fill my whole soul. My dreams of ministry appeared to be dashed forever.

Though, given what I'd witnessed over the years from those "saints," I believe I'd rather be a "sinner." I've learned that those people would make the homeless a sandwich but wouldn't sit with them to eat it. They want people who don't go to church to not swear or do drugs or drink or anything else "bad" before they'll tell them about the love of God. Nope, good people live under a rock. And I wanted nothing more to do with them.

"Alright, enough for today. See you tomorrow." I patted his head.

"Naw, church." He struggled to stand up, his giggles still going strong.

"Oh, of course. I forgot." I held out my hand to help him up.

"Ya gotta come." He flashed me a smile. "Or my granddaddy gonna show up here."

"Why is your grandfather so bent on me going to your church?" I turned from him to start picking up the tools.

"Easy. He the pastor. He wantin' everyone there." Hank handed me a few items and then headed out the door. "See ya tomorrow. Jesus love ya. I love ya. Flyer on ya bed for church." He waved his arm then pounded on his chest as he bounded down the steps.

No, just no. Church was part of the old life, a life when I'd done everything right and it'd still turned out so wrong in such an epic way. There was a whole series of events in my story I wasn't about to tell anyone. I wandered over to the porch steps and sat down, watching the world around me as I slipped into musing about my past life.

***

All those years ago, I lived a life where I tried to audition for the role of pastor after graduation … and failed in grand style. I didn't fit the mold, not one iota. Oh, I went to those interviews at churches all prim and proper. Greeted by people who looked down their noses at me from the start. They wanted nothing more than to grill me about my personal life.

"So, Miss Smith. What are your plans for marriage and children?" this rather overbearing pastor asked. He sat there in his two-sizes-too-small suit, eating his third donut. "Being a children's pastor is a big responsibility."

I looked down at my hands, twisting my clenched fingers. Gazing back up, I said, "Oh I love kids, I've learned all about the proper way to incorporate play into learning –"

"Yes, yes, but you need to have your own child to fully understand children," another man from the church council chimed in.

"Well, I hadn't thought much about marriage and having kids." I tried looking at the only woman in the room, hoping she'd throw me a lifeline. No luck. All she did was bring in more coffee before hurrying back out.

"But a single woman can have so much temptation," another man with a stain on his tie added.

I took in a deep breath. *Okay, here goes nothing. I'm going to try some honesty.* "I'm already married but children are out of the question."

You guessed it, this led to other questions I had no answers to.

"And why is there no mention of a husband? Your home church pastor and the church you interned at both stated you were single," the pastor said.

"He's not a churchgoer." I gulped, unsure where this was going.

One of the council members raised an eyebrow, leaning as far forward as he could. "Well, how do you expect to get others into the pews if you can't even get your own husband to attend?"

And I was out. They weren't going to hire me. Every one of the interviews went almost like that.

After about a half dozen or so of these interrogation sessions, I was done. My soul left in shreds from these so-called "men of God" who wanted nothing more than to tear me down. A small part of me believed they might've been right. How could I stand before a church full of people when I felt like the biggest sinner in the room?

I hadn't remained pure – I mean I had these thoughts sometimes that were less than clean. I'd broken more than a few of the commandments, at least I felt like I had. And most of all, I didn't act like anyone else in church ever did. I listened to music they never would. I read books they never would. I no longer wore dresses every time I went to church. I spent a whole lot of time hanging out on the wrong side of town in places "saints" weren't supposed to go. Oh, don't get me wrong. I wasn't going into the bars to have a drink or two. I was looking for Tom. Okay, it started as that, but it ended up as something else entirely. So many people need a helping hand.

And worst still, I was a horrible helpmate to my husband the few times he did show up. Yeah, after a while I gave up and didn't even try. Tom was so overwhelming; I never did find a way to cope with him. Not even a little bit in all those years. Yup, I helped others but never the one person I'm sure God had put specifically in my path for me to support.

So, yes, I continued to work as a secretary for that firm I'd worked for during college. However, the duration turned out to be only for a short time after graduation. But it wasn't the dream job I'd hoped for. My great boss got pregnant and quit without warning. My new boss ended up being an idiot of a man, and I discovered this my second day as his assistant.

Yeah, that guy was one of those slick dudes who thought they were catnip to women. However, he wasn't all that great. Short, stubby little man with a circular bald spot that he tried to hide with a bad combover. One lazy eye, and both were a weird shade of greenish-grey. His suits were always wrinkled and his shirts stained with something gross. He reeked of too much Old Spice; I could smell him from down the hall. When I'd been assigned to him, I almost quit on the spot. Still, I needed money so much that I couldn't even consider doing something so foolish.

So, there we were that Tuesday. The phones rang off the hook as they always did, and I did the best I could to answer all of them, read the mail, make copies, and do whatever else. Then he popped his head out of his office, and I started to gag from the stench.

"Hey, hon, I need you to get me some folders and tabs from the supply closet." His lips curled up as he tapped on the doorframe.

Trying not to roll my eyes at this ridiculous interruption of my morning, I stood up. Walking as quick as possible the few feet to the closet, I sensed someone was behind me. Ignoring that feeling, I entered the tiny space. Someone followed me in and closed the door behind us. Because the smell of cologne didn't fade, I knew it was my boss. Crud. Why bother to ask me to come in here if he was just going to come as well?

I started to turn around, but he shoved me against the wall. My cheek ground into the rough plaster as he tried to wriggle his fingers under my shirt toward my bra and into my pants. Every ounce of me suffocated, for a second, I couldn't breathe.

But as I struggled to find my voice to scream, I found my strength instead. I fought back. It wasn't right for him to be doing this. I wasn't having anything to do with him, this situation, or anything. It didn't take me long to twist around enough to give him a hard slap on the face. And he gave up. For the time being.

"Ah, the rough stuff is nice," he snickered as he approached the door, rubbing his jaw with one hand and the front of his pants with the other. "But if you want to keep your job, tomorrow show up in a skirt and looser underwear. No, scratch that. No underwear at all." He spun his head toward me, licking his lips before biting them. He arched his back as he released his grip on his pants. Then he opened the door and sauntered out.

Leaning against the wall for a moment, I wondered what I should do next. As I put my hand up to my face, I could smell him on my skin. No, no job was worth this. I could find another place to work where I wouldn't be groped by some slime bucket of a man. I'd quit. Yet, my gut told me that wasn't the right course of action. I hadn't done anything wrong here. My boss had.

Thus, I marched right down to the manager's office to complain, every inch of me on fire. Ready to announce to the world what a cad this man, no, what scoundrels all men were. I was out for blood, his head on a pike, a burning at the stake. However, all my righteous indignation got me exactly nowhere.

I opened the door to the manager's office, he looked up at me from his desk with a giant question mark on his face. Before I lost my courage, I spat out, "Hey, I just got told that I need to come to work tomorrow without…"

The odor of my boss's cologne wafted into the room, followed by my boss with his fat lip. "Whatever the girl told you just now is a lie. Look what she did to me."

The manager spun his gaze from me to my boss and back again. Without asking for more information, he said, "Amy, you're fired. We have a no physical violence policy."

"But –" I started.

"No, get your things and get out of the building before I have to call security." He started to stand.

I pushed past my boss, looking at my feet, not at him. Hoping for all the world that his next secretary would turn out to be a man.

Thus, I ended up with a string of odd jobs, easier to cope with somehow. Babysitting, dog walking, house cleaning, you know, those jobs that only teenagers want. Most of them paid in cold hard cash so I never paid taxes. Heck, I didn't even file the forms for years.

Don't judge me.

As far as I was concerned, it was a hear no evil, see no evil, speak no evil state of affairs. I wasn't going to ever be asking for any government handouts; thus, Uncle Sam and I had no beef with each other. And my little pile of cash grew quite fat, but that's much later in the story. And something I was never going to tell Hank or anyone, including my son. Oh, that money I buried deep. And I do mean that in every sense.

After my popup husband had stolen money from me twice, I needed a strategy to protect myself in all ways from all comers. The first time he made off with my money, well, I never was sure he'd actually done it. The wedding money was gone in a puff of smoke, and I never asked questions.

But the second time, oh, I knew beyond a shadow of a doubt what had gone down. I'd walked in on him with his hand in my purse, pulling out my envelope of cash. And my wallet with my driver's license and social security card. In the blink of an eye, he ran out my door. Yup, after that, my determination to never let him or anyone else touch my stash ever again became rather an obsession. Goodness me, I was just like a pirate hoarding her treasure.

One lesson I learned early was I had myself alone to rely on. There is no fallback plan, no running home in tears to hide in the woods, and no man to lean on. It seemed that my father was the only decent guy on the planet. Oh, and Ike. But I wasn't about to abandon everything and live with a homeless man. To this day, I've never had a clue if my parents were ever aware of how strong of a child they raised. To them, I'm sure I looked like a drifting weed blown every which way.

Because for quite some time, I didn't remain in one spot for long. Okay, I stayed in the same state, however not the same place. Not on your life was I going to stay tied down when I didn't have to be. Lived in a travel trailer for a long time after I finished college, enjoying every little camping nook I could find.

It was wonderful and, yes, I do think in the back of my mind part of the reason I did so was to make it harder for Tom to find me. What to do with my wayward spouse always left me feeling conflicted. Help him or not? The effort it took to be his advocate was so much more than I ever bargained for. So, yes, in the early days, I wanted to be the wife he needed. Later, not so much. By the time I'd bought the camper, my life was almost my own at that point. However, there was someone else I felt the need to protect much more than Tom.

And over the years, I found ways to help others. Little things for the most part. I'd sit with the homeless on the street corners and listen to their problems. Why? Easy, to find ways to help them where they were at. Oh, I'd met many who wouldn't ask for what they needed but if nudged in the right direction would take it. I'd volunteered for everything I could find – soup kitchens, neighborhood associations, community development councils, the women's prison, you name it. If someone's house burned down, I'd be the first one there with the offer of help. If someone had a baby, I'd be on the phone calling everyone to make sure meals showed up. For years, I did lots of little stuff like that, and I was happy to do so.

Not that I'm asking for recognition. Far from it. Most people had no idea of all the things I involved myself in. Jesus said to go out into all the world and love the unlovable, like the woman at the well. Or the unwanted, like the lepers. Or the hated, like the tax collectors. And that's what I did. Who needed to be a pastor in the official sense to preach the love of God? Not I. Heck, those church people wouldn't even let me teach Sunday school.

Because the biggest thing I'd learned in life was that religion and faith weren't the same thing. Not even close. Faith was between my God and me alone. I didn't need a third wheel telling me what to believe or not. Or people telling me what rules to follow. My faith was as strong as ever, even if I never darkened the doors of a church ever again in my life. Yes, I'm aware that many feel this is breaking a commandment – keep the Sabbath holy. Me? No, a building isn't required to honor the Sabbath. I could worship my God on a hike. Or in silent prayer and meditation from almost anywhere. Much better than trying to listen to God while sitting next to someone who wants nothing more than to gossip about you later.

Yeah, I get it. I'm a square peg and didn't fit in the round hole of what a Christian should look like. Image was the end-all and be-all to those "saints." The heart meant nothing. Thus, I drifted further and further from the church. Doing what I believed to be right, following my own brand of faith, and doing my best to ignore the "saints" who whispered lies about me.

Chapter 15

Interrupting my reflections, a deep voice, way too close to my ear, boomed out words I didn't comprehend. My shriek filled the air and my body landed hard in the grass. Looking around, I was almost surprised to find I wasn't in my home state. Don't think I'd ever been that lost in thought before. Yet here I was, with Jessie hovering over me.

"Whoa, didn't mean to make you jump out of your skin." He placed a bag and a tray with two cups in it on the porch. "I said 'hi' twice before I got close. But you were out in space I guess." He grasped my elbow with his gentle hand, pulling me to my unsteady feet.

My eyes blinked faster than hummingbird wings, making it hard to focus on anything. My heart hurt it raced so fast, and the tingling in my toes wasn't from my fall, I was sure.

"Yeah. Planning my next move is all," I replied.

"What? You giving up already?" He chuckled as he sat down, legs stretched out and ankles crossed. He leaned back, grabbing one of the drinks and taking a slow sip. "I know I've been a bit cross with you when I've talked to you in an official capacity. Sorry, nature of the job. But I didn't mean to scare you off. I've tried to catch you again at the coffee shop but no such luck there."

"I've been busy. Thanks for stopping by. I do believe I need to get back to work now." I grimaced. This guy had an answer for everything it seemed.

"Ah, and this is our first date. You can't leave yet." His eyes, soft pools of brown, stared at me as he cocked his head.

A gulp stuck in my throat. I began to cough and then snorted as my weak knees gave out and I sank to the steps. No, no, no. My nose started making that dreaded pig snort I do when I'm nervous or upset. And right then, I was both.

He handed me the other drink; I took a swig of what turned out to be some of the sweetest tea I'd ever tasted. Resulting in me doing a spit take.

Well, these actions will put the whole "dating" idea out of this foolish man's head.

My mind drew a complete blank as to why he'd shown up here and think I'd be fine with sharing a meal with a strange man.

He clapped my back a few times. "Gosh, I must've really startled you. Okay. Let's start over again. My name's Jessie. Let's pretend we've been set up on a blind date. I'll take the food and drinks round back to your table and then come back for you. Sound alright to you?" He gave me a quick wink and a half-grin.

There wasn't any way I could do more than nod at this point, oh, and give a hint of a smile as I looked up at his kind face. He was a few years younger than me from the looks of things. I spotted a few wrinkles on his dark face. His deep chocolate eyes almost lost under his bushy black eyebrows.

The other times he'd stop by he'd been wearing his uniform. However, today he wore faded jeans and a dark green polo shirt. I guess I hadn't stopped to observe him before, either here or the brief encounters at the coffee shop. All I'd seen was the uniform, not the man. Not the bulging muscles against the short sleeves. Not the face which now looked at me with a mix of kindness and worry, the eyes crinkled, the lips pursed. Not the hands which now reached out to hold mine, rough, strong, steady hands. As I released him to walk toward the backyard, I watched him march in a precise line beside the house. Ramrod straight, rock-solid, and so like my father I wanted to cry.

This was the type of man I should've married.

Shivering at my thoughts, I turned to follow. I rounded the corner of the house and took a moment to gaze at him as he set out our dinner. It felt nice for someone else to be taking care of me for once. My gut twisted in knots, not sure if I should continue with this, whatever it was. I'd been so rude to him the other times we'd interacted.

Plus, men weren't good news. They've always led to ruin. Connections have caused nothing but my downfall and a whole lot of heartache. Yet, I took a few steps forward, holding my breath and clenching my fists.

"I'm Amy," I said, managing to squeeze these words out of my dry mouth.

He turned toward me, holding out his hand. "I know."

Firm and tight, he seized my hand in his and pulled me the rest of the way to the table. "I'm so glad you decided to come." His smile could've set the world on fire.

"Uhm, yeah." I sat on the edge of my seat.

He handed me a wrapped sandwich, a bag of chips, and my drink. He plopped down on his chair, digging out his food. "So, where ya from?"

"Not here." I munched on a chip, not sure how much I wanted to tell him. My whole body now so tense even my toes were curled.

He whistled, low and soft. Eating for a minute he scanned me up and down. "Miss Samuel can't wait to see what you've got planned for the place. Do you have a color scheme in mind?

Gonna keep the same layout?" He tipped his chin my way before taking a sip of his drink. "I love the detailing on the porch, don't know who taught you woodworking, but you're amazing at it."

At his praise, I calmed down a bit. A flash of my father and I in his workshop flooded my brain. Some of my best moments had been there as a child. "Thanks. Colors are rather eclectic. Yes, same layout – two bedrooms." I took a deep breath. "My father taught me everything I ever needed to know."

We chatted for a while more about the house. The place was our only point of reference after all. Light, easy conversation. But I was no longer the naïve child I once was, the one who'd gotten married on a whim. A song flitted through my head, "Then you smiled and I reached out to you. I could tell you were lonely too. One look, then it all began for you and me." No, life and love weren't that easy.

"Amy, have you thought about staying somewhere else until you're finished?" Jessie began to pick up all the trash from the table.

"No. You never complained again after I ordered the shed. Figured I was good." I slipped my hand on top of his. My fair skin glowed against his darker tone.

"Sort of. You were smart to put the door facing away from the street. That way I can't say anything about it. But I'm not super comfortable with you staying here." He made a slight move with his hand to clasp mine.

"I'm good, but thanks for asking." Not like he'd asked. Yet, I guess this was to be expected. He was doing his duty.

He reached over, putting a finger on my chin. I turned my head a bit to shake him off. That felt like too intimate of an act for him to do on a "first" date. He pulled his hand back in a fist, glancing over at the house.

"Alrighty then. I probably should get going." He stood up so quick, the table wobbled. "Have a great night. Hope you've got a lock on that thing." He shook a finger toward the shed.

"Yeah." I giggled, a stupid little schoolgirl sound. Flipping my hair around in its ponytail, "Good night. Thanks for dinner."

"Good night." He grabbed the trash and strode off.

The next morning, I again lounged at the coffee shop. Taking a few slow sips of my coffee, I ignored my pastry and wondered what to do about Jessie and our "date." When you got right down to it, I believe it'd been my first date ever. Because somehow, I don't think the non-event of having fries while discussing wedding plans with a stranger quite counted.

My breath came out in a low groan. My gut told me the right thing to do was to shut down whatever this was with Jessie. My son needed to be my top priority. Well, after I finished the house and I had some stability in my life again that is. Plus, based on the other morning, I was sure Jessie was one of those religious people I tried to avoid. I shouldn't have led him on the night before.

"Hey ya!" A male voice broke into my thoughts.

Ugh. *Why did people keep interrupting me like I didn't have anything better to do than drop whatever I was doing to dote on them?* Looking around with glazed eyes, I squinted against the bright sunlight streaming in from the window.

Oh, great, perfect. Here I was thinking of Jessie and poof, low and behold, standing before me was Jessie. *Why wasn't he in church?* His clothing made it look like that's where he was going, yet here he was. *Wasn't last night enough?* No, I'm not responding. Yikes. That's going to seem so rude after our chat and dinner.

Didn't matter about my hesitation. He sat down opposite me while I still debated in my head, tapping his fingers on his leg, beaming from ear to ear, and not caring in the least I remained silent.

"So, I went to the early service today, hoping to catch you again. Guess you're not a churchgoer. That's okay, I guess. Or maybe you haven't found one yet." He nodded several times, his eyes getting bigger. "Oh, yeah, that must be the case, what with you being new in town and all. Great. So, yeah, would love for you to join me sometime. We have awesome music. Well, you heard some of it the other night." He looked at me, again waiting for me to say something. "The preacher isn't half bad; he can be a mite long-winded at times." He chuckled.

All the air in me came out in a long, slow sigh as it hit me. Never once in all my years had men found any sort of attraction to me. Yet, somehow, in this new city, I'd discovered a man who appeared to think the best flower to draw all the bees in town was me.

How was that even possible? Sweaty men are supposed to be hot, not women who perspired over every inch of their being. No, as my mother would say, "Women glow, dear." Even then, it wasn't something that was pretty to look at.

Nevertheless, I did look for all the world to be a damsel in distress. Here I was out in public, sitting in cut-off shorts and a t-shirt with holes in it. Both also had paint, grease, and who knows what else on them. My hair pulled up in a sloppy bun, dirty and shaggy. Perhaps that's where the appeal was. Helping the little, fragile woman before she killed herself.

Clutching my cup with both hands like a life preserver, I took a stab at letting this guy down gentle enough he wouldn't end up with a bruised ego. "Hold up. Let me stop you right there. I'm thought about this, and I'm not interested. You hear me?" My lips pulled in tight, and my eyes narrowed in my effort to not glance up at him.

"In church or me?" He straightened up as much as he could in the chair, his body tense waiting for the answer.

Oh, my goodness. This guy was worse than a dog with a bone. There weren't any options at this point. I was going to have to find a new place to hang out.

"Either," came my curt reply.

"Oooh, this is going to be fun. I'm going to wear you down. Everyone loves me! You'll see." He chuckled as he stood up. "Until next time." With easy strides, he walked out the door, not waiting for any response from me.

Wonderful, now I had a stalker. What else could go wrong?

Chapter 16

On Monday, Hank showed up as always. Not a word about not seeing me the day before. We worked for a while in silence before I broke into the quiet. "Hey, want to hear what happened next?"

"Ya betcha!" He gave me a spurt of handclaps. All smiles and grins.

"Well, I rather gave up after that fiasco. Oh, I know I shouldn't have, but I did. Time marched on and I just left things to stew." I pressed my lips together, letting my thoughts cement for a moment before pushing on.

***

And life continued on alone. I did what I had to do, nothing more. I became lost in my own little world of work, school, and work some more. There was no getting out of the crazy spiral, well, not until graduation. Oh, how I dreamed of that day. The glorious day I'd be granted the opportunity to go out into the world and say, "I'm Pastor Amy…"

Would I have worked myself to the bone if I'd known that day would never come? Hard to say.

Kept going to school. Kept busy with work. Kept dwelling on the fateful Tom Disaster Day. Yes, I'd made it a permanent holiday in my head. You know, like the Great Chicago Fire. Or the Blizzard of '69. Stupid, yeah, I hear you on that one. But until the completion of the remodel on my apartment and I could move back in, that day stuck with me. The motel dive had been a wonderful diversion from reality, thanks for asking. Who needed a television with the neighbors screaming at each other at all hours of the day and night? Which was so easy to hear with the paper-thin walls in the place. The water in the shower ran boiling hot for all of a minute and then freezing cold for the next two days. And the motel sign lit up my room blinking on and off every five seconds like clockwork.

Maybe after I had my own space again then the last time I'd seen Tom would seem less like a momentous event. Until then, I lived in an odd dream world.

I often made the rounds of the bars, looking for Tom; they were the only places I could think of that might sell drugs. Yeah, I know, bad idea. But marijuana doesn't fall off trees you know. Tom had to find his supply from somewhere. However, I was too much of a chicken to ask the sketchy-looking guy at the truck stop if he was a dealer. Yet, my gut told me the man was up to no good, for he stood there every single day in the exact same spot. Okay, rather, he leaned on lamppost in the far corner of the lot.

In the fall, my apartment was ready for me again. I moved back in without any hesitation, so happy to be home. I'd been watching the progress as it crawled along as I had to go there every few days to pick up my mail. I'd never imagined the project would take nearly six months.

The library at night had become my favorite place during those months. A place I could be alone with nothing but my thoughts and books. Lots and lots of books. Books are the best friends to have. They don't judge you. They can take you to places you've never been before. They may smell weird sometimes. Yet it's comforting in the same way your grandmother's peculiar scent is. Best of all, they wait forever for you to come to them. Standing on their shelves, they hope you'll find them. That you'll pick them. That you'll want them.

So, there I was one night, well past ten, and still in the library. The long shadows from the fading sun had disappeared faster than the airhead co-eds hours ago. Nothing left but a few dim bulbs, a few nerds, and me. Working on a paper for finals… well, that had been my goal. But I scribbled on my notebook instead. Lots and lots of flowers, birds, and other hideous doodle art covered the page.

Yeah, the last two hours had been so productive. Not one book cracked open. The whole stack perched there on the edge of the desk like a mocking Leaning Tower of Pisa. Fine, so sometimes books in a group are judgmental. Alone, they don't seem to have that kind of power.

My pager vibrated again. Never should've gotten the darn thing. Since it could only be my mother, I didn't bother to turn it over to see what the message said. She'd called a million times today. And yesterday. And the day before that. Yes, I'll admit, I'm dodging my mother. Have been for almost a year now for several excellent reasons.

Not like it mattered. My mother was in my brain. You know how it is; she was always ready to make me feel guilty over every little thing I did…

"Why would a nice girl like you wear that blouse? You can see everything."

"Is that lipstick the right shade for you? You look like you work in the world's oldest profession."

"Are you avoiding me? You never call."

"Why did you have to move so far away? The other side of the state, really?"

"You're breaking my heart when you don't call every day…"

I could go on, but you get the kind of hamster wheel thoughts whirling around in my head.

Truth be told, I couldn't begin to fathom what to say to her anymore when she called. She'd been so happy that my "special someone" had been found. Then I never mentioned poor Tom again. Not one single time since I moved away and started college the year before. I had even gone so far as to keep our conversations short. And I do mean short.

As in, "Hi, Mother. No, I haven't fallen into the lake and drowned. Bye." This was simple to do, because I didn't dare risk seeing her face to face again. No, I could never have stood up to that scrutiny. One quick glance from my mother and she'd comprehend the whole sordid situation. And she'd be able to do that without me saying a word. Mothers, go figure.

Yup, easy as pie, all I had to do was never ever go home again. Fine by me. I had nothing to brag about at the next high school reunion. "Most likely to marry the Invisible Man" wasn't in the yearbook.

Yeah, yeah, Tom wasn't invisible. But he might as well have been. I saw Ike more often. You may wonder, well, couldn't my parents come visit me? No, and I can thank my lucky stars all day long for that. My mother, at our tearful goodbye, acted like I was dying.

She's lived in the same tiny cabin for most of her married life. As far as she was concerned, the best thing she'd ever done was to leave society. She'd always said that people weren't kind to strangers in other places. It was so much safer, nicer, and simpler to stay in the same place, forever, and ever, amen. I never asked her what happened to make her feel that way. Still, I'd seen pictures in a secret box she'd hidden under her bed. Photos from somewhere beautiful with palm trees. And of a man who wasn't my dad.

Thus, for her, my moving halfway across the state might as well have been to the moon. I'd promised Tom and I would come back for the holidays. And for all summer. After all, his job required travel, so we shouldn't be tied to one place, right? But I'd up and got married to an insane man, so now I couldn't go home again – ever. All because I couldn't admit the truth of how weird of an existence I lived. That there was no "we" in this marriage. No, only me.

Somehow, not having a perfect marriage would let my parents down. Okay, I know everyone had the sense something was off about the marriage from the beginning. But Tom hadn't done any damage before I moved – only after. And there was the giant lie I'd told about Tom having a job in this college town. I couldn't undo that, no way to walk that back. Plus, I hadn't succeeded in finding him again. I had to wait for him to come back from whatever "trip" he was on. Whatever info my parents already had was all they were going to know.

So, I'd missed the holidays. Literally. I couldn't bring myself to celebrate alone. You don't cook a turkey for one person. Then you'd have to eat turkey and only turkey until the next Thanksgiving. Yuck. And you don't give yourself gifts. Thus, Christmas had gone out the window as well.

Then I'd missed summer. Instead of hanging with my parents, I stayed on at my job because Tom still hadn't reappeared. My boss was so happy to have me not disappear when the school year was over. I was one of the few full-time employees she had who was also a student. Yes, I now worked full time, saving like mad to move into a bigger apartment. And pay for help from a professional for Tom.

Because if Tom ever came back, he needed to have his own room. No way would I sleep in the same room with him, marriage or no marriage. And his room was going to have a lock on the door. Not the standard lock where he could lock himself inside. Nope, I was going to turn it around so I could keep him *in*. Don't ask. I recognized how bad of a plan that was. Trying to keep the wind prisoner wasn't going to be easy.

However, getting Tom to actually visit a psychiatrist didn't appear like it was going to be a walk in the park either. Still, without him showing back up all my plan were pointless.

Now winter had almost arrived again, and I was still in my freshman year of college since I was only going part-time now. Thus, I hadn't finished all of my first-year courses by the end of spring but would by the end of this term. At this rate, I might get lucky and finish college before I turned thirty.

Yet according to everyone, this was the best time of my life. If you asked me, I would've disagreed. After all, take into consideration the anchor I had tied around my neck. Still… Tom still hadn't shown up again as I thought he would. One lousy night. That's all my marriage was. One lousy night in more than a year. Or was it two nights? There were those few awkward moments in his truck on our wedding night.

So, sure, my marriage may not even have been legal. We'd never formalized anything. Oh, but don't forget the incident with him in the buff…

My pager vibrated again. In my haste to grab it to turn it off, I hit the edge of the pile of books. They fell to the floor with a crash, all thirty or so of them. Looking around, I couldn't see anyone in my immediate area who might've heard. Not caring anymore, I gave the books a hasty glance to see if any of the pages were crushed. Not seeing any major damage, I left the whole lot of them in the heap where they lay. The librarian was blind; he wouldn't have a clue who'd been the culprit in leaving the mess behind.

Grabbing my stuff, I proceeded to sneak out of the library like a thief in the night. I'd gone so far beyond little-miss-goody-two-shoes in one short year it was beyond scary. Wasn't even sure why I still went to church at that point. Or still went to college. God knew all about what I'd been up to. Telling lies, flashing my undies to the world, insurance fraud, dishonoring my parents, and who knows what else.

Arriving back at my apartment landing, I saw a huddled form leaning against my door. The bulb remained burned out up there. No, it hadn't been fixed during the remodel. Go figure. A sudden gust of wind almost knocked me back down the stairs. Shivering at the blast of cold air, I pulled my coat tighter.

This was the worst game show ever. Door number one: face Tom and another disaster? Or door number two: go back down the stairs, hop in my car, drive around the block, and camp for the night?

But my one and only mentor, friend, guru, and guide, Ike kept reminding me that marriage was for better or for worse. Despite me not being as faithful to him as I should've been. Oh, I know, most of these acts of infidelity were in my mind and nothing I'd ever acted on. However, my father's words still rung in my ears – the thought and the act were the same.

Add the fact I'd tried for a second or two to find my erstwhile husband, and now I had. There really was only one choice here.

Door number one it was. Yet, no way would I ever let Tom out of my sight. No way to skate out of destroying the apartment twice.

Ugh. I'd have to even drag him into the bathroom with me. Double ugh. And my bedroom. That was beyond ugh – all the way to I'm going to hurl. But, hey, now that I thought about it, this meant I didn't have to work quite so hard. I didn't need the bigger apartment after all because locking him up was never going to work no matter where I lived. He'd wreck every room he was in if no one kept an eye on him. Yeah, everything came down to me. I'd have to watch every little move he made. Unless a good psychiatrist could find a way to get him to be less destructive.

Walking the short distance down the landing, I tried not to make a sound. It was like trying not to step on bubble wrap without the gunshot effect. Each footfall seemed to thud or thunk as I tripped all the way down. The noise echoed back at me from the surrounding buildings. Boy, I needed to start channeling my inner Ginger Rogers right about then. Ball, chain, slide, cha, cha, cha. Or whatever.

The lump moved as I drew nearer. I could now see eyes as the whites glowed in the dark. "Where in the hell have you been? And why don't you ever answer your pager anymore, young lady?!" The form resolved into my strait-laced, uptight grandmother as it rose from the floor. Layers of clothing flew off in all directions like falling leaves in the autumn wind.

In what seemed like only a moment later, my grandmother sat beside me as I reclined on my almost new couch. She patted my hand, cooing over me like I was five. If you must know, that was the time I had fallen out of a tree and broken my arm. It was the only time she had acted like a caring grandmother and not a harpy. Her actions now soothed and comforted me for about ten seconds. Right up until I figured out it wasn't some weird dream.

My grandmother was, in fact, in my living room. Thus, I must conclude her swearing and rising like a ghost of Christmas past was real too. Oh, I'm in sooo much trouble now. Even Tom would've been a better surprise than this.

Grandma looked the same as she always had. Immaculate short bob for her frosted grey hair which was always done in the latest style. No wrinkles on her face, thanks to one of the best and expensive plastic surgeons. Oh, and lots of concealer. Her dress a soft grey knit with a cream belt and matching wrap. Sensible cream flats on her tiny little feet, and pearls dangled in her ears and from around her neck. The modern version of June Cleaver, the same as my mother. Who else could still appear that amazing after rising out of a pile of laundry? She looked as if she'd left home but a minute ago.

"Oh, wonderful, you're awake. You hit your head pretty hard when you fainted. Did you eat enough today? Your blood sugar is probably low. I'll see if you have some juice. You're so skinny. You look worse than a waif begging on a street corner. Don't you eat anymore? Where's Tom? Boy, you two keep odd hours. I've been here since a little after six this morning and look at how late it is now – almost midnight. I've been sitting on that hard concrete landing all day, no food, no water. Well, that Mrs. Diaz next door did offer to let me relax in their apartment. Thank goodness I understand a bit of Spanish thanks to my maid from Guatemala. Uhm, or is it Honduras? Whatever. That's not the important issue here." She waved her hand in the general direction of the apartment next door.

"But of course, I refused. I'm not entering the home of a maid, not for love or money. Why didn't you tell me you lived in such a bad neighborhood? I mean, honestly, dear, are you the only white person for ten miles or what? When was the last time the outside of this building was redone? 1950? I swear I saw bullet holes in the side wall. At least your apartment looks like it was remodeled this decade. And the paint in here looks new, like maybe a few months old. Honey, I would've sent you enough money to get a real apartment and not this slum if I'd known. I always knew you'd end up broke or worse. Oh, and the appliances in the kitchen look new also. You never share with me anymore..."

Taking in a deep breath, she wound up for more. More badgering, more guilt, more shame thrown down upon me like hail from above. Hail that would kill me if I didn't find a way to dodge it in the next second or two.

I wasn't going to respond to most of what she'd said. "Grandma, Tom's working out of town right now. Mom never mentioned you were coming when we spoke last week. I'm busy with finals."

I bit my lip. My eyelashes whipped back and forth as the moisture from my eyes leaked out of the corners. Pressing my fingers into my eyelids, I tried to calm down. Shock, not blood sugar caused me to blackout. Not like I'd ever tell her that. But now my anger started to grow.

What in the world was she doing here? Oh, my heavens how much does she know? My grandmother swears?! Blinking a few more times, I looked her right in the eye. Like I would a bear before I shot it.

"Well, I wanted to surprise you. I couldn't be there for the wedding since you didn't bother to invite me. How bad is this guy? Never mind, I can only guess since your father –" She drew out the word "father" so long, and yeah, I've always known how she felt about him since she never said his name. "– picked him. Not like you ever sent me a thank you for the wedding gift. So, I thought I'd throw you two crazy kids a one-year anniversary party. Well, a year and a half party. Is that too much to ask?" Her hands raised in a surrender gesture but that wasn't what she was doing.

She had thrown down the gauntlet; she was daring me to show her I'd married the perfect gentleman. She had also chucked in as many guilt-inducing statements as I'm sure she could think of. Her face contorted into a picture of a puppy kicked two seconds ago and a newborn lamb. *I'm so dead.*

Yes, it was too much to ask. An anniversary party would require both Tom and I to be there. "I don't have time for a party, Grandma. Plus, I'm not sure when Tom's assignment ends." I rose to her challenge – part truth and part lie.

"But I came all this way...." A single tear escaped her left eye.

She turned her back to me as she dug in her purse for a tissue to wipe it away and sniffle for a moment. This was the full-tilt "poor, pitiful me" mode that both my grandmother and mother are famous for. Men melted when these two powerful women did that.

Oh, and as the story goes, men have also mopped the floor with their bare hands to make them happy again. However, this emotional form of blackmail from both of them had never worked on me. Why she thought it would work now I didn't understand.

"So why don't you go to your hotel and we'll talk more in the morning?" I clenched my teeth at my grandmother's back. But the pain in my jaw was so not worth the effort it took to not start screaming.

She took a deep breath in, "What hotel? You think I would book a hotel? Why waste all that money? Do you know how much the flight costs? And I got the cheap one. I left home yesterday morning, flew to New York. Then Boston. Then Chicago. Then Atlanta. Then Dallas. Then Des Moines. Then LA. Then Las Vegas. Then Phoenix. Then Seattle. Then Denver. Then here. Then I sat outside your door all day. I've been up for almost forty-eight hours."

She patted my arm and continued, "Show me to your guest room and let me have a little nap. Then I'll clean this place top to bottom. Really, now that you're a wife, you should be doing a better job at keeping your home clean. It's the first thing I noticed when I walked in the door. Dust, dirt, grime. Oh, my, gracious. And I was dragging you and my luggage in with me. What must your guests think?" She fluffed her hair and pulled on her belt for a second. "Even you were taught better than this, I'm sure."

Her eyes darted around the apartment. Carrying out an in-depth scan for every microscopic bit of dust and cataloging them for later, when she'd show each and every one to me. After she had swept them into a humongous pile of course. And to think, my mother was even worse than this so many times. And my mother lived in a cabin in the woods not in a mansion in a city.

Taking a moment to center myself, I had to wonder at a few things. Based on the rant, I now had a complete understanding of where I got my penny-pinching and cleaning habits from. Made me feel a whole heap sorry for whoever my grandmother's current maid happened to be. But I had to form some kind of a response to all of this without being rude or letting a whisper of truth about my marriage slip out.

"First, there's no guest room, so you have to sleep on the couch if you're sleeping here. Second, you're my first guest ever, so I have no idea what guests think. Third, my apartment isn't dirty, so don't clean it. You know as well as I do Momma taught me everything I need to know about cleaning. Fourth, there's nothing wrong with the neighborhood or my neighbors. You should know better; you come from a real city with real crime and poverty, not a little hick town like this. I live here because the rent's cheap, and you should know, Mrs. Diaz isn't going to do you any harm. Fifth, if I lived in a better neighborhood, you'd never have been able to camp on my doorstep all day. Sixth, who takes two days to fly all over the country to save twenty dollars on airfare? That's rather dumb, Grandma." Glaring over at her, I half hoped she'd disappear.

I pushed myself off the lumpy couch. Stomping off to my bedroom, I slammed the door as heat burned in me.

"So, the party's still a go then?" My grandmother's voice wafted to me from the other room. "We can't have it here, that's rather obvious. Everyone will find out you can't take care of yourself. Is your church an option? Or is it in this horrible neighborhood too? I'll make sure your parents save the date! I haven't seen them in ages. Why doesn't your mother ever visit me? She's my only daughter after all."

There could be no response from me that would appease my grandmother. Thus, to the beat of the tom-toms in my head, I took a migraine pill and flopped onto my bed.

In the morning, there wasn't any option but to face down my grandmother. I told her in no uncertain terms to leave. Dealing with finals and a party was simply too much for me to handle. After mumbling a few words about a discussion with my mother, to my surprise, she acquiesced. Do believe she'd been told a few things about my husband I'd have rather been kept secret.

Chapter 17

Tom did show back up again, sooner or later. He'd stay a night or two, wreak havoc, and disappear again. This would happen several times over the years. I'm not sure you could say love grew, but my heart did soften toward my spouse. More pity than anything else, I'd guess. I tried to talk to him about getting the proper help or maybe start taking some type of medication. His response was always, "There's nothing wrong with me!"

Thus, I tried counseling him myself. After all, I was learning more and more how to do this in my courses at college. Yikes, don't even get me started on what a disaster trying to psychoanalyze your spouse was. But, yeah, I now understood why doctors don't treat family. I was too involved, too invested in the whole situation to ever be able to disconnect emotionally.

And yes, at some point, I did change my name. However, I very seldom gave that name except in those times I felt a legal obligation to do so. You know, like when I bought a car, rented an apartment, or opened a bank account. But no, I never did start wearing that symbol of marriage on my hand. My ring remained buried in the bottom of my jewelry case in my drawer. My inner conflict over my marriage became impossible to resolve.

In due course, we consummated our marriage. It was inevitable, I suppose. There were times when Tom would show up being charming, funny, almost normal. My shock could be seen from the moon, I'm sure. I'd play along, and I'd ignore what he acted like most of the time. Oh, I know, even those times he acted "normal" never ended well.

Like the night a few months after I graduated, the night I conceived my son. Don't remember what odd job I had at the time, but the events of the evening are seared in my memory. I'd returned home and was starting to cook dinner, when a quick rap on the door interrupted me.

Rushing to answer it and not caring in the least who it might be, I pulled it open. There stood Tom in a black dress shirt and a bright red tie. Neat as a pin. And his eyes clear as glass. A bouquet of daisies held in his hand, and a wide grin spread across his face. "Happy Valentine's Day, baby!" He chuckled as he shoved the flowers my way.

Those were the first and last flowers my husband ever gave me. And the fact he'd remembered something romantic was a miracle. For a flash, joy filled me. My world filled with warmth and light, brushing the darkness from every corner. That little nugget of hope buried in my heart pushed to the surface. Every little thing was coming up roses for once.

"Wow, thanks," I gushed, gesturing for him to come in. Not caring in the least that the day was, in fact, February 13th. And a Friday no less. "Have a seat, I was making dinner, but I can adjust things so there'll be enough for both of us."

I placed the flowers in a cup on the side table by the couch. We stood for a moment, gazing at each other. Those awkward few moments we always seemed to have each time he showed up again. He took my hand, giving it a gentle squeeze.

"Great, thanks." He slipped his arm around me and kissed me on the cheek. "I've missed you, girl. We need to spend more time together; you make everything better." He rubbed my back in small circles.

"Then don't leave." I grabbed his face with my hands. He smelled nice, musky. Not a hint of marijuana or booze – like he would on a normal day.

He pulled me onto the couch with him, heavy petting became so much more. After we were done, we snuggled against each other for what felt like forever. He played with my hair, humming to himself. This was comfortable, nice and what marriage should be. Not the craziness we had most of the time.

"I'm hungry; go finish dinner." He swatted my stomach, giving me a push.

I threw my clothes back on, not thinking anything about his last remark. Went back to the kitchen and did the last little bit of cooking. As I brought out the heaping plates of food, he looked up at me from the couch. He continued in his state of nakedness, reclining as he watched my every move.

"I'll stay if you start being a better wife. You're not a very good cook, you know." He rose with a slow graceful stretch, walking over to the table. He sat down, covering his nude form partially with his napkin.

I placed his plate in front of him without a word. I didn't need to respond; I could see where this was headed. I joined him, playing with my food, not eating. My heart broke into a million pieces. In less than an hour, he was back to "normal." There was no getting off the roller coaster that was my marriage.

He ate in silence for a few moments before dropping his fork on the table. "What is this? There's worms in here!" He threw the plate against the wall with a loud crash. I watched as the stroganoff slid down to the floor. A slime trail of noodles, grease, and sauce left an odd pattern against the beige paint.

He stood up, grabbed my plate, and smashed it to the floor too. Next, he marched into the kitchen, and the sounds of breaking dishes and the ting of metal echoed back at me. I didn't move, not wishing to be in the line of fire. I simply stared at the stain on the wall. A plate whizzed by my head, hitting the wall beyond me with a clatter. Flinching, I switched my gaze toward the entrance to the kitchen.

Tom sauntered over to his clothing and started to yank on his things. He pulled out a small bottle from the pocket of his pants and took a swig. "Well, you going to get up and make me something edible or not?" He swiped his mouth with the back of his hand.

Still, I remained frozen. Unwilling to do or say anything, hoping the moment would pass, knowing with every ounce of my being it wouldn't. This was Tom in all his glory. Manic, depressed, happy, sad, relaxed, angry, high, or drinking. Often all of the above at practically the same time. When I didn't move, he left without another word.

A few months later, I confirmed my pregnancy. Not something I'd ever expected given the hit-and-miss nature of our relationship. Tom was nothing more than a figment of my imagination as far as I was concerned. But I welcomed the blessing of a child. It made my life and marriage more real somehow.

And rumors swirled around me once I started to show that infamous baby bump. For the most part, I ignored them. I just didn't care what people thought about me, where they thought my child had come from, or their opinions on how I chose to live. And this is when I stopped going to church for all intents and purposes. Those people didn't want to help a young woman with child. Or at least not one who for all the world looked like she was going to be a single mother. Oh no, they just wanted to know who the baby daddy was. Not my fault I didn't want to play their sick game.

Problem was, most of the odd jobs I found were from people in the church. My source of income dried up rather quick. Which made me surer I was correct in my thinking; religion wasn't part of God's plan at all. Because the Bible says to 'visit orphans and widows in their distress'. Yeah, I know, I wasn't a widow in the truest sense. However, I was in need, and these dear "saints" had no interest in helping me one tiny little bit.

So, I did what was required of me. Stood on my own two feet, took care of myself, and brought my child into the world with no assistance from anyone. You're right, my parents more than likely would've welcomed me home with open arms. Still, I wasn't going to go backward in life. Too many things were getting lost along the way, and my word wasn't going to be one of them. I'd made a commitment to marriage, and I would stick with it – for better or for worse.

Sometime after my son Paul's first birthday, a day came when I guess everything became too much. Not for me, but for Tom.

He'd popped in, unannounced as usual. I answered the door to find him standing there a bit disheveled and with a puzzled look on his face. "Hey, honey. Why'd you move?" He leaned on the frame, tilting his head down toward me.

I'd moved to a downstairs apartment after Paul was born, same building, but a place with two bedrooms. "Come in, we need to talk." I tugged on his arm, not wanting this drama to play out in front of the neighbors.

As he entered, Paul started to howl from his playpen in the corner.

Tom jerked, blinking owlishly. "What the…" He crept toward the sound. "Get this thing out of here! Now!" He put his hands over his ears, staring down at our child.

I curled up my lips. Oh, this so wasn't going to be easy. Though, so not my fault my husband hadn't know about my pregnancy or the birth of our child. As slow as possible, I walked over to Tom and pulled his hand down. "That's a child, not a thing. His name is Paul; you're his father."

He spun around, bolting for the other side of the room. "Not possible. No way. The meds..." He pounded his fist on the wall.

Uhm, I do believe I'd misheard something. I'd never seen him take medication, only drugs and alcohol. Skipping that slip of the tongue, I replied, "No mistake about it, Tom. We made a baby." I picked up my little bundle of joy, cooing so he'd settle. I breathed in deep the scent of baby lotion, spit-up, and dirty diaper. "I need to change him. Don't move, I'll be right back, okay?"

Those few moments I was in the other room, my heart raced out of control. No doubt, Tom had fled the scene by now. Why wouldn't he? But as I returned to the living room, there he still was, huddled in a ball in the corner. And I made the biggest mistake of my life.

"Would you like to hold him?" I walked over to Tom, kneeling before him and holding Paul out for him to take.

Tom peeked up at me through small slits and opened his eyes a bit more as he lowered his gaze to what I offered him. He held out his hands. I placed my child in those waiting arms. And in a flash, Paul began to wail.

Tom leapt up, shaking Paul hard. "Do these things only scream?!" Tom continued to shake Paul, and Paul yelled louder. I tried to wrestle my son out of Tom's firm grip.

And then, Tom dropped Paul onto the hardwood floor with a dull thud. Silence washed over the room. As I reached down to scoop up my child, my heart sank. I'd allowed someone I knew was a danger to himself and others to hold the most precious thing in the world.

Tom ran out the door, leaving it open in his wake. I sank to the floor, my tears falling onto the bundle in my arms as I inspected every inch of him. In a moment or two, his cries started up again. For all the world, he didn't look any worse for wear – a few marks from Tom's tight grasp and a few red spots which I was sure would turn into bruises. Still, I didn't take any chances. Nope, I rushed straight to the pediatrician's office, sounding like a madwoman as I demanded they examine my son that instant.

In those moments at the doctor's office, I became aware life wasn't about me anymore. Protecting my son was a bigger priority than helping my husband. Tom had gone a step too far. Yes, I understood he had an illness. But that didn't give him a free pass to do anything he wanted to do. And hurting a child was so off-limits.

In the next few weeks, I changed my whole life. Gave up the apartment, sold the Bug, bought a truck and camper. Sorted through everything I owned and decided what was a need and what was a want. Ended up giving away most of what I owned. You just can't take much with you when you live in a tiny nineteen-foot trailer, you know.

Thus, I lived my life how I saw fit as I raised my child. We developed friendships of a fashion and built a world for the two of us. All without worrying too much about what my husband was up to. Therefore, my unusual lifestyle didn't affect anyone but my son and me. So, living in a travel trailer for a few years looked almost normal. My son loved the adventure of pulling up stakes and seeing somewhere new all the time. And it made homeschooling a bit more fun. Odd kind of childhood for him, I suppose, but it was him and me against the universe for the most part.

The only true connections we kept were my parents. We'd stop by the ranch often. My father taught my son to be a man - hunting, fishing, you know, the kinds of things men should do. I was only too happy to hand my son over to my father for a few days of male bonding. Sure, this left me stuck with my mother and her endless questions about where my husband was. While I never did quite compound my first lie with a second, I also wasn't forthcoming with the truth either. Omission remained my best friend.

My father, on the other hand, never said a word about Tom. And I never found the courage to ask him the big questions. You know. How did they meet in the first place? And why was this man my perfect mate?

But my father did mention on more than one occasion that Paul was the reason for my marriage. Still and all, I wasn't sure he was correct on this. There had to be something more than just my son for it to be worth all the effort involved.

Without any goals, I became aimless and wandered. What I'd always wanted in life wasn't to be - a good wife, a pastor, safe, settled. So, I settled for nothing in the end. No real job, no worries, no problems. Don't get me wrong; I worked and I worked hard. Sheared sheep in season, delivered newspapers for a spell, and took people to the doctor. I specialized in side gigs before they were a thing. I had one rule: I had to bring my son along with me no matter the task. We were a package deal. And I made more than I ever dreamed I would.

Sure, a part of me still had enough faith to want my son to have this grounding as well. No matter the fact we didn't have a "home base" so to speak. I made it a priority for him to be in church and made sure he was part of the children's choir, Bible quiz, and youth group. I stayed off to the side, out of the line of fire as best I could. I only hoped my son didn't hear what those other mothers were saying about us. Because learning about Jesus shouldn't have to come with a side dish of gossip.

But those little needles hurt. People claimed I begged for money or clothes for my child, and there were the never-ending remarks about my son being a bastard. Of course, rumors swirled around about what the inside of my trailer looked like. Goodness only knows what I was up to in there.

Don't get me wrong; church folk aren't the only ones who love inuendo and flat-out lies. Oh, golly gee no. I heard these backhanded comments from people in the grocery store, the banks, and the campgrounds. And more than a few people who hired me for jobs did so for the sole purpose of prying into my private life. Not like I ever once took the bait; I smiled and nodded in the face of any and all comers.

But it gnawed on my soul that my son might be hearing it all as well. And this was where my biggest failing as a mother was: not sitting him down and telling him something. Yeah, looking back on everything now, I so wish I had. But you know the saying, "If wishes were horses, beggars would ride."

In my thirties, my father died of a heart attack. He passed out in the woods and faded away, alone. His faithful dog alerted my mother of trouble, but by then, it was too late. He was long gone. My mother and I left to scatter his ashes along the trail he loved to stroll on each morning. Both of us said not a word as we completed our task, watching the ashes float on the wind to land among the tall grasses and the pine needles.

A month later, my grandmother passed away as well. And much to my shock, she left me a rather sizable chunk of money. Oh, and a note that read, "Dear, I know you never amounted to anything. But your son needs a life even if you refuse to give him one." Yeah, there was more, however, I didn't bother to read it. Why bring more nonsense into my life?

At that point, I decided some roots might not be such a bad thing. No, I don't think it was my grandmother's words alone that did it. My son was twelve by then. He needed more than the wandering life. He should have friends and things he could call his own. Maybe go to a physical school with the other children for a change. Thus, I bought a house. All in cash, which didn't even put much of a dent in my stash. This turned out to be a mistake.

Because, you guessed it, Tom reappeared after over ten years of being gone. As I sat on the front porch one morning, sipping my coffee and reading the paper, I spotted a man strolling down the street. I was hit with a weird sense of familiarity. I knew this man but from where? Then he opened my front gate, taking those few steps up my walkway. It clicked; Tom was here. So ashamed to admit my first thought was that I was glad Paul was gone for the week with some friends.

Tom stood before me, no scruffy beard, no shaggy hair. His soft grey t-shirt was clean, and his jeans didn't have a hole in sight. His eyes swept over the front of the house before landing on me. "Well, you did good for yourself." He started to come up the steps.

"Don't." I stood and moved toward him, every ounce of me on edge. "Not until you tell me where you've been all this time." I wasn't sure if I was angry, in shock, or hurt. Or all of the above and more.

"None of your darn business." He inched a bit closer to me, his face stern and tight.

It wasn't like I'd ever been able to find out where he lived when he wasn't with me. Yet, this was a lot more years than he'd ever been gone before. I grabbed onto the pillar, digging my nails into the rough bricks. Did I want to start an argument about who and what he was? Not in the least. "Fine, what do you want?" I huffed out, exacerbated at the insanity of it all. My life, his version of reality.

"To see my son." He rubbed his hand on the stair rail, gazing down at his feet for a moment then back up at me.

Yeah, no way, no-how buddy. "Why? After all this time? You've never been here for anything! The one time you saw him, you totally freaked out. What's changed?" I cringed at the thought of explaining Tom to Paul. Never once had I answered any of my son's questions about his father. I'd even gone so far as to tell my parents not to say anything about Tom as well. Which, between you and me, is beyond awkward to ask your parents for.

"I have. I go to a good doctor now and try to take my meds all the time. I'm ready." He crossed his hands at his waist, lacing his fingers.

"Paul doesn't know about you." Honesty is the best policy. Even when the truth hurts. "He's not ready." I swallowed hard.

"That's not fair. I'm his father. It was your job to tell him!" He bounced on his toes.

"Do you know how old he is?" Enough already, I was keenly aware of what my job happened to be. Being a mother had nothing to do with telling your child about why the other parent was absent.

"Uhm…" He backed up a bit, almost falling as he hit the edge of the step. Adjusting himself, he ended back up on the walkway. One hand stretched out, clutching the railing as if he was trying to pull himself back toward me. "That's not important. You can't keep me from seeing my son."

"Don't have to. You've been doing fine with that all on your own. Now, I'm happy you're finally getting the help you need. I'd love to have a chat with your doctor. Later, we'll figure out the best way to introduce you and Paul." I gave him the best smile I could under the circumstances. What I really wanted to do was scream at him, tell him to get the heck out of Dodge.

His eyes drilled into me for a moment, then he charged up the stairs. He shoved me so hard I fell against my chair. He rushed to the door, yanking it open. Running into the house, he began to yell, "Paul, Paul!"

Leaping up, I followed him. "Calm down! Paul isn't home." Though, I so wished our dog had been about then. But where my son went, his dog went as well. They were inseparable and had been since the day we'd brought the puppy home.

He spun around, grabbed me, and shook me hard and fast. I tried to free myself, his fingers digging into my flesh tighter no matter what I did. We did this crazy dance around the living room for a moment or two, as I struggled to push him away. In the end, I landed a knee where no man wants to be hit.

He threw me to the ground. "You lying slut. I've been doing everything right and still you don't want me!" He gave me a swift kick in my side.

My breath came out in a whoosh, pain filling every inch of me. Nope, he was wrong, nothing had changed. Curling into a ball, I inched toward the nearest corner. Sliding into a seated position, I glared up at him. Back in the day, fighting him made him angrier. Being passive had been the only way to go.

I let out a slow breath, releasing as much tension as possible. Wiggling my fingers and toes, while trying to focus myself. "Hey, everything's fine. Take a good look around the house. You'll see I'm telling the truth. I'm here alone. Then we'll talk, okay?" I watched him stalk around the room like a caged cat for several minutes.

Without another word, he stormed out the doorway. I stood to watch him as he continued his march down the street. Heaving a massive sigh of relief, I hoped this was the end of things.

No such luck there. The next morning, I prepped my coffee as usual, ready to start my day on the porch by watching the world go by. When I opened my door to go out to snag the newspaper and sit down, there was Tom, relaxing in my chair with not a care in the world. He was smoking a joint like the old days. With stubble from an unshaven face and the same outfit from the day before.

"Hey sleepyhead, glad you finally decided to join me. Paul right behind you?" His head did a slow pivot toward me, his eyes landing on a spot well past my shoulder.

With great trepidation, I slid over to the other chair and plopped down. So much for my calming morning ritual. "Put out the stupid cigarette. This is a nonsmoking house." I opted to stare at the lighter winking up at me from the table rather than him. Gold with the emblem of an eagle embossed on it, much too fancy to be something Tom would've bought. Almost asked him if he'd stolen it.

"Were you always such a goody-goody?" His loud cough made me glance up. His hand waved smoke away from his face. The joint hung loosely in the fingers of his other hand as it draped over the side of the armrest.

"If you don't put that out, I'll put it out for you." My fingers started to snake toward the vile thing.

"Whatever. It's calming you know." He smushed the butt against the wall of the house, leaving a streak of ash. "My son?" He leaned over, picking up the lighter. He flipped it open and closed. Then he flicked it on for a second, watching the flame with some intent. Then he pinched it out between his thumb and forefinger. He turned his eyes to me again. "My son?" he repeated.

Ugh, he had such a one-track mind. "Still not here." I tapped on the armrest and then switched to biting my nail. Trying to figure out how to get the name of the doctor who was treating him without another angry outburst. But for the life of me, I didn't see how avoiding Tom going postal was possible.

"I need to see my son!" He jumped up, the chair flying backward.

I froze, the rage came much sooner than I'd anticipated. Not good. No way to stop this train. "I understand, but there are certain steps that have got to happen first." So proud of myself. I hadn't flinched or reacted in any way.

"You'll pay for this! You wait and see!" He waved a finger under my nose, leaning down almost an inch from my face.

When he got no response, I guess he felt he'd made his point. He took giant strides out of the yard as I sat watching his retreating back.

And the lyrics of a song hit me, "When everything falls into place like the flick of a switch, well my mama told me there'll be days like this." Yup, I was back in the old cycle of things with Tom. I'd been fortunate over the last few years to have him leave me alone, safe and untouched. But now, he was going to start popping back up again. And there was only one thing he wanted this time: to hurt my child. My stomach churned and not because it was empty.

And I, like a fool, went about my morning like I was a normal person. Instead, I should've called the police and reported a threat on my life. And on the life of my son. But, nope, I ran errands without a care in the world. Only to come home to a street full of firetrucks. All my neighbors from the block were standing there, watching the show.

Upon seeing me, everyone started asking me if I was okay and where Paul was. I tried to be hard, strong. Not let those people see me cry. As I watched the final mop-up, I realized what roots I'd planted were gone.

Yup, I lost everything in a house fire. And I do mean everything. Well, I did find a knife which was salvageable under a corner of the rubble. The real peculiar thing was, no cause of the fire could ever be determined. The fire marshal wouldn't even hazard a guess, because there wasn't anything left to sift through to get any clues from.

Yes, the fire looked odd to everyone. The blaze burned so hot and fast that from the moment the neighbors called 911 to my house being a pile of ashes was something like thirty minutes.

And this wasn't a cheap trailer, mind you. No, this was a solid brick and mortar house which had stood the test of time for almost a hundred years – until I had become the proud owner. And Tom showed up, of course.

Oh, you know I had my suspicions from the get-go. There was so much history with Tom, my home, and fire. Plus, there was his not so veiled threat shortly before my home was destroyed. Add to that, the day after the fire, I found a cigarette lighter in the backyard. Not just any lighter, no. I found that fancy one Tom had on my porch. A bit singed, dirty, and marred. However, I knew the thing the instant I spotted it lying there. But I never acted on my doubts. I never even let out one tiny little hint. I just felt so blessed no one was there and no one was harmed. Stuff wasn't what was important in life. Everything was replaceable except for my precious child. And he was safe.

Chapter 18

And life continued on for a few months. After buying another house, I developed a vigilance for security. My home must be watched at all times. By me, my son, our dog, a camera – didn't matter. By then, the internet was a thing, and I found ways to earn money online. Wanting my son to always be close, I went back to homeschooling him. Things were safe, settled, quiet. Oh, I still did my many little tasks for the community and the less fortunate.

My mother died in her sleep about three months after the fire. With no warning at all, I got a call from a neighbor who had brought her breakfast. Nothing anyone could've done. She was there one day and gone the next. My world shrank down to nothing fast, giving me no time to dwell on all the death around me.

Not like there were many people in my life to begin with. I tried to keep myself apart from most. Wagging tongues were my constant nemesis, as they had been for years, which is why I didn't visit my hometown often. Or go to church much. Or develop deep friendships. My little bubble of a world was safer.

There I was, walking that trail in the woods again and sprinkling ashes again – this time I had no one to lean on. I left the dust of my mother to mingle with the forest and the remains of my father.

No, I didn't allow my son to be part of either time I scattered the ashes of my parents. While he was close to both of his grandparents, unlike I'd been with mine, I felt this was a burden for me to handle. Paul sat beside me at the church memorial services for both and then went with a friend for the rest of the day. Allowing me the time to privately say my goodbyes.

Later in the day, as I cleaned out my parent's cabin in the woods, I found that wooden box under their bed, the one I remembered from when I was a small child. I sat on the floor and poked through the contents. Inside were a few mementos of their life together – photos, love notes, you know the kind of thing. And I found those other photos I'd seen earlier, the ones with the palm trees. As I looked closer, I wished I had some idea where the beach in the photos was and who the man was. Because he gave my mother a look that was rather similar to the one my father always gave her. This man was in love. However, there wasn't anything written on any of the pictures.

Maybe my parents' perfect marriage wasn't as wonderful as they had made it appear to be. I'd been striving after an impossible ideal to live up to. My failures weren't mine. Yet, I didn't have the time to dwell on it.

Weird letters began to show up around this time, they started shortly before my mother's death. Collections accounts for bills I didn't know I owed. Why would I need a diamond ring? A vacation in Hawaii? Or a fancy new car? I called them up and, as polite as possible, explained that these were a mistake, but I got nowhere.

Then calls came in for Tom, and they wouldn't accept my little lie of an answer of, "I haven't seen him in years."

They'd always replied something to the effect of, "He's your husband."

Well, by that point, it was in title only. Not like he deserved the title.

With each new call, something in the back of my brain nudged at me. Trying to make me remember something. Still, no matter how hard I tried, the image never became clear. One thing I knew for a certainty: I didn't use credit of any kind.

And then came the phone call which explained it all. "Hello," my chipper voice answered the line, a normal day in my anything but normal life.

A high-pitched squeak demanded on the other end, "Don't mess with my husband anymore. And stop demanding child support for a child you don't have!"

"I think you have the wrong number." I started to hang up. I wasn't going to deal with whatever this was.

The woman on the phone hissed loud enough that I could hear despite the fact the phone was almost back in its cradle, "Nope, you're Amy Smith. I've got the right person."

I tapped my nails on my teeth. If she knew me, why didn't I know her? "And you are?" Okay, I'll bite and play the game for a minute.

"Stella Smith. Your hooks can't be in my husband anymore," she barked.

"And your husband is?" Oh, I was so afraid of where this was going. But I had to ask as my body tensed so much I rose half out of my chair.

"Tom Smith. As if you didn't know. He said he told you we were getting married when you got divorced." She huffed several times, her breathing painful to my ears.

Yikes, the train wreck ended up so much worse than I thought. When had the two of them gotten married? Silly me, I had to ask. "And when was that exactly?"

"Duh, as if you don't know. He said you were dumb, but geez, you sound like a fruit loop. We got married about fifteen years ago." A dog barked in the distance as she spoke.

If her wedding was that long ago, we'd been married to the same man the whole time. As in, within a year or two of each other. But why was she calling me now after all these years? This made no sense to me. The blood swished into my head, ringing in my ears. It started pounding out a rhythm that my hand began to mimic as it gripped the phone even tighter. "Okay, listen. Tom Smith is a common name. There's got to be some sort of mix up here." Even my toes curled in anticipation of the answer, breathing impossible.

"No, no mix up, you idiot. He's been all excited the last few weeks about meeting his kid after all this time and getting back together with you. Why you made this up after all these years and why you want him again is beyond me. Just stop. I finally got him off the drugs and to go to a doctor. And now this...." Her voice trailed off.

Oh, my gosh. She'd called the right person. And this was a nightmare, but it explained a whole lot. "My son is twelve. I'm not divorced. I never asked for child support. The last time I spoke to Tom was a few months ago, and that didn't end well." Each simple sentence spoken as slow and drawn out as possible. Trying to make everything as clear as I could in a very muddy situation.

"You're lying! You can't have a kid!" she screamed as she ended the call.

I spent the next ten minutes screaming and beating up every pillow on my office couch. This couldn't be real; I'd waken up in the twilight zone somehow. For reasons I couldn't explain, this other woman was the one my husband had chosen to be with. Lyrics popped into my head, "Why not me when the nights get cold? Why not me when you're growin' old? Why not me?" What made her better than me? Why hadn't I tried harder to help Tom the few times he popped in? No. That wasn't a road I was willing to walk down.

Don't know how long my rage would've lasted, but a quiet little voice interrupted me, calling out to me from another room.

"Mom? You okay?" Paul hadn't knocked on my office door. He knew better than to interrupt me when I was working. Yet, I didn't start yelling on a normal day.

I replied without opening the door, afraid my face would betray me, "I'm fine, honey. I need to wrap some things up. Sorry. Sometimes even adults have to vent. I'm going to shut up now."

About an hour later, I noticed a popup on my computer screen – an email message. From my new best friend Stella. How in the world she got my address, I'll never know. It read:

> Sorry, I got so upset. Bit of a shock and all. Didn't mean to make you mad too. Turns out Tom's been using social media to talk to your child. Seems he kept both of us in the dark. No problem. We'll adopt him and you get a divorce. Everything's gonna be great. Talk soon!
> 😊 😊 Stella

I wanted to hurl. Her solution was me giving up my child? What kind of lunatic was this woman? No, no can do. And I now understood my son's sudden fascination with his phone. He'd made a new friend. Here I thought he'd been chatting with his buddies from those few months he'd been in school. Oh no, my husband had done an end run around me. I wanted to kill the man I'd made the mistake of marrying.

Without any hesitation at all, I called an attorney. Who wasn't in any rush to make an appointment to help me with a divorce. And then I phoned the police. Who were only too happy to file a report about a bigamist. And to learn about someone who may be using my social security number to obtain credit.

Because, after I'd calmed down from my phone conversation with Stella, something had clicked. I remembered my stolen wallet all those years ago. Tom knew my social security number. Rushing to my computer, I found a way to pull up a credit report. Not something I'd ever done before in my life, yet now I majorly regretted not doing so sooner. Yeah, the evidence was all there. Pages and pages of addresses, various types of credit and so much more. Tom, or someone, had been pretending to be me for years.

This was a man who was going to destroy me. Worse yet, he was going to destroy my child. Both of my parents were now dead. There wasn't any reason to hold onto the last rule I still kept – that marriage was sacred. Divorcing someone in these circumstances didn't appear to be such a bad thing. Because right at that moment, my gut feeling was my marriage had never been part of God's plan at all. The only good to come from my life had been my child, and adopting a child would've been so much easier.

I made the mistake of telling a few people I'd filed for divorce. Yes, this would've ended up as public news at some point since the local paper puts divorce notices in when they become final. In my small town, those tidbits of sensational news take off like wildfire. With about as much scorched earth left behind. In my case, I didn't wait for the inevitable; I opened my mouth early. However, despite me never once saying the exact reason for ending my decades-long union, rumors flew. About a man none of them had ever met and few even knew existed.

Oh, and the tales were whoppers. Yup, one said my husband had been jailed for any manner of crimes. Or he was a Muslim and lived in another country. Or, well, whatever. I stopped listening to the wild yarns being spun rather quickly. Okay, even I didn't know the real truth about my so-called husband, thus any of them might've had some basis in fact.

Not all of the stories were about my other half, heavens no. I found out that my son was the result of my numerous affairs – which I never knew I had. Or that the reason I lived in a trailer for so long was I was a lady of ill repute. Gracious, how anyone one could think either of those things when I never even looked at men was beyond me.

My reputation lay in tatters, and I was no longer welcome anywhere. It turned out to be true, divorce was one of those unforgivable sins. Or maybe, the sin was keeping my private life private for so many years. Thus, there wasn't a grain of truth to start any of the rumors on.

Yet, I never discussed any of these matters with my son, Paul. Even though I cringed every time I thought about what his father might be telling him in those private chats. My big fat mouth was going to stay shut on the matter. I'm not one to gossip, not in the least little bit.

Still, somewhere deep inside me, I was aware Paul wasn't my little boy anymore. And this became obvious in the most painful way when his beloved dog died a few weeks later. Oh, she'd been sick for quite some time, and we knew it was coming. But she was part of our family, closer to my son than a sister. Therefore, we made the difficult choice to have her die at home in her dog bed by the fire. It was her favorite spot after all. All for the plan, our vet agreed wholeheartedly that it was the best for everyone.

Sitting on the couch that morning, I remained silent as I gazed at Paul. He rocked her head in his arms, and as we watched the life drain out of his pet, I wanted to stop the world. Go back in time and start over again from several years ago. Paul would still have both his grandparents and his dog. And some of the craziness wouldn't have ever invaded my life. But there was no going back; life was a one-way street.

After the vet left, I wrapped up the lifeless corpse in an old blanket. "I'll do the rest, honey. You go to your room and watch some TV. You relax for a while." Giving him a brief hug, I tried to smile without bursting into tears. He didn't need his momma melting into the floor.

"It's my job, mom. She's always been my responsibility. I'll dig the grave and bury her." His head bowed, not even looking up at me at all.

So I stood at the kitchen window, watching him as he completed the task. His strong back to me, his shoulders hunched in sorrow. Even from this distance, it was clear his knees were buckling every few minutes from the weight of his grief. Nevertheless, the mound of dirt beside the hole did get bigger, inch by painful inch. And as it did, he began to stand a bit taller, a bit straighter, his legs a bit stiffer. This was his rite of passage into adulthood, no matter how hard it was. For him or for me.

Because there was nothing I wanted more at that moment than to run out to him and take all of his pain. To put it onto my back instead. Each agonizing second ripped a new piece of my heart out of my chest.

This event turned into the catalyst for telling Paul about the divorce. For letting him pick a side. Thus, at some point soon after I had filed for divorce, I came to the conclusion I should give my son the choice. He'd shown me he was adult enough to handle a life-altering decision such as this: live with me or live with his father. My heart told me there really was only one option here – me. I'd raised him, been there for him every moment of every day.

And he crushed my heart. My son and I had the famous all-out screaming match. He claimed to know the truth about my marriage and his father. Therefore, I'd been lying to him for years. Though, based on what he said, he knew nothing except a bunch of lies and half-truths his father had fed to him during their few brief messages online. I alone knew the truth because I'd lived it. I knew what had happened and I knew I'd never spoken about his father even once.

Because I never had a clue what to say. How do you explain to a child their father was paranoid? Or did drugs to cope with mental illness? Or disappeared for years with no good reason why? Or wasn't there for his child's birth? And what kind of father was never there once for his birthday? Or for Christmas or any holiday, for that matter? Or any other important moment of his life?

No, I wasn't going to give any sort of answer to Paul. Not then, not later, maybe not ever. I didn't care what manner of filth Tom spewed out. The truth would stand in the end if I found an ounce of bravery to speak up. Because I wasn't going to twist anything to fit anyone else's narrative. And if my son never came to see that, that was on him, not me.

Yeah, Paul chose his father over me. This new person now featured so prominently in his life and filled in the gaps I'd left with my silence. Leaving my heart aching over the fact this might destroy the bond I had with my darling son. He'd been my whole world for so long. Before the divorce was even final, off he went to live with total strangers.

Chapter 19

Shaking my head, I forced myself back to the present.

"I do believe I never should've started telling you this, Hank." I sat with a heavy thump on the floor. Tears started to roll down my cheeks. My wails rose and fell, echoing in a crescendo around me.

Looking around me at the disaster that was my life, I now understood where I'd made my mistake. From the words "I do." No wait, it was much earlier than that. I've never done a single thing right my whole life and never would. Ugh. Because I'd tried too hard to follow the rules and stay on the straight path, I'd ended so far from where I ever thought I would ever be. I was fundamentally flawed somehow.

"I'm a-gonna get my uncle." Hank patted my head as he walked by.

Of course, he didn't know what to do with a hysterical female. He was only a kid after all.

I wasn't aware of when the two of them came back. But at some point, the arms of a man wrapped around me.

"There, there, Amy. Everything will be fine. Put your trust in Him. Hank told me a bit about why you don't believe anymore, but He's still there. He never left you, even if it seems like He did." His voice soft, low, and calm in the face of my storm. And the voice seemed so familiar. I knew this person.

All the while, I blubbered like a baby with my head buried in my arms. My face wet from my tears, slime coming out of my nose, drool running down my chin. My mother would've killed me. You can't entertain guests in such a state. However, stopping wasn't possible. And this man's words were no comfort because I knew he was wrong. My faith had gone out the window with everything else in the last few months. No, I'm sure my faith had left even before that.

I couldn't see answers coming from all those years of believing something better lay right around the corner. Not when what waited around the bend got worse each time. No, I could keep getting whacked only so many times before I no longer had hope in a better day. Before I no longer believed in a higher power who controlled our lives. Trust me, no genie waits around to grant wishes to those who ask.

"Tell me what brought you here, Amy. Hank told me a bit of your story. But a sticking point's somewhere, yes?" His gentle, strong hand held mine. Turning my head, I took a peep at who held me. Jessie. Jessie was Hank's uncle? Yet, somehow this fact didn't matter. Yet it did explain so much.

But, no, I wasn't going to give in. This can of worms I should've buried long ago. Too many what-ifs, should've-dones, and regrets to ever look back.

"Too much water under the bridge." Feeling it best to keep it simple, I wanted to leave it at that. But the pain inside me had grown so much stronger now than ever before. A living, breathing thing trying to escape.

"You can't keep everything bottled up. Your heart's telling you to spill. This is why you told Hank so much. Finish your story. With me, with Hank, with someone. It doesn't matter." He tapped his fingers against my palm, slow and rhythmic. "You can't heal until you do."

"I lost my son! I just let him walk out of my life without saying a word!" There was my fatal mistake, the moment my world crashed to a halt.

"Somehow, I believe there's more here than that. The way you treat Hank... well, you stepped into his life with such kindness." Jessie rubbed my shoulder, soft and slow.

I clicked my fingernails together. The sound annoyed me, it grated on my nerves. Yet it made me feel better somehow. At some junction, I feared I was going to have to explain to my son what his father was. Not a conversation any mother wanted to have. "Even my son doesn't know all of my reasons. Although, I do believe he has an idea."

"And why do you think that?" He grasped my hands to make them be still.

Biting my lip, "Because before I moved, I found out he and his father had been having conversations online. And his father told him to keep them secret. Uhm, I didn't stop these chats. And then I was an idiot and let my son decide who he wanted to live with. He didn't choose me. Now he's there, learning what my ex-husband is like in all his glory. Oh, my goodness, you wouldn't believe what chaos that man is capable of creating. But if I'd only called the police about my suspicions before I heard from that woman...."

I gulped in a huge amount of air before exhaling. I'd made the man sound like some kind of monster. Okay, he was a criminal, but only technicality. Oh, my word, why was I trying to justify his actions again? Like I had for so many years?

"Do believe I need some notion of what you mean here." He gave me a look. You know those looks of confusion when a piece of the puzzle is lost and gone forever. Yeah, Jessie didn't know about a lot of things in my life. Plus, he was a cop.

"Well, I guess I need to finish the story." And so, I began again with my heart in my throat and rocks in my stomach.

***

Adrift on a sea of doubt as to what I should do with the rest of my life, I went numb after I lost my son. My child had been my anchor for far too long. Floating all I could do, as I struggled to keep my head above water. I hid in my house, waiting for the saga of the divorce to be over. I guess I should've moved then.

During that time of waiting, so many decisions begged for my attention. Do I press charges for the bigamy? Do I press charges for the fraud? Do I just do the easy thing and get the divorce? In the end, I did what I thought was best for my son. Dropped everything but the divorce. My child didn't need a parent in jail. About a year later, I became a newly minted single woman at last, untangled from my marriage.

Oh, but that final decree wasn't easy to get as all that. No, way, no how. I walked into the court at the appointed time, wearing a dress for the first time in years. Ready to sign papers and be done with the mess in two seconds flat. I entered an almost empty room, even so, I sat in the last row. My back ramrod straight, my hands clasped in my lap, my head down. A man wearing a robe entered, carrying a stack of papers under his arm. He settled himself behind the bench not looking out into the room at all. My name was called. I rose to my feet and took a few hesitant steps toward the front.

The judge glanced up at me then back at the papers in front of him. "Mrs. Smith?"

"Yes." I rushed to finish the last few feet so I stood before him.

"I'm a bit confused here. You stated on the paperwork you haven't lived with your husband for over ten years. Is that correct?" He tapped on the file with his finger.

"Yes." I bit my lip; I recognized this wasn't normal. Though, I wasn't going to explain to this man how I hadn't wanted to disappoint my father. How I'd wanted to keep my commitments. How I'd believed I had done what God wanted me to do. And how, in the end, I'd married a man who might have burned my house down. Yet this same man had somehow managed to win the heart of my son.

"But he visited you and your child, correct?" He flipped a paper.

"Uhm..." How do I answer that? In the office before being sent in here, I'd been told to tell the truth. And that I had to answer every question the judge asked. "Tom visited me a few months ago. My son Paul wasn't home at the time."

"Okay, let me see if I've got this straight. You and your husband separated over ten years ago. He's only visited once since then. And you just filed for divorce last year?" He rapped on the desk with his knuckle. "I'm sorry, but something about this isn't adding up. While this isn't a criminal proceeding and you aren't technically under oath, you do need to be honest here."

Crud. So much for just signing a few papers. "My husband suffers from mental illness." I twisted my hands, crunching my knuckles.

He didn't respond for a few minutes as he read over the paperwork and ignored me. Looking back up, he wagged a finger at me. "Yet it states here, you agreed to your husband having full custody. Please, Mrs. Smith, help me understand what is going on here."

I closed my eyes, trying to settle the butterflies in my stomach. If I didn't have a complete understanding of the whole situation, how could I explain it to someone else? "I allowed my son to choose."

"Why?" His question rung out in the room, hanging in the air for a moment.

I pursed my lips, opening my eyes I looked straight up at my accuser. "Because I *knew* he would pick me. But I was as wrong about that as I was wrong about everything else."

There were other questions, so many questions I'd been trying not to ask myself for years. I tried to keep my answers as simple as possible. No way did I want to be responsible for my soon-to-be ex-husband going to jail. Not after everything I'd done to keep him out. For years.

In the end, the judge agreed to my demands for everything. He cleared me of the debt. I got my name changed. I was responsible for nothing my husband had done.

As soon as I got home, with my divorce papers clutched tight in my hands, I called a few women who might still be friends. I wanted to invite them to my house for a party. None dared to answer the phone, return my messages, or show up. No matter. I was going to make it a night to remember anyway.

At that party of one, I burned my marriage certificate on the top of a bonfire out in my backyard. Don't ask me why that silly piece of paper remained in my life, kept safe and sound inside a safe deposit box for years. Drank enough lemonade and ate enough appetizers to make myself want to throw up.

And then I turned my back to the largest, previously blank wall in my living room. Making a bunch of wishes for good luck, I closed my eyes and threw a dart at a blown-up map of three states in the south. A giant map I'd made at the local print shop the day before. Why those states? It was the farthest place I could think of from where my now ex-husband lived. Not like I didn't want to visit Paul. Or make it harder for him to see me. Still, my heart told me it would be a long time before that bond could be rebuilt.

The next day, I bought a house sight unseen in the nearest town to where the point had landed. More of a city, really, on the coast at the opposite end of the country from where I'd always lived. Then a short time later, I stepped off a bus in my new hometown. No faith, no marriage, no family, no friends. New everything. Every string that had ever anchored me to the earth was gone.

During the year I was getting the divorce, I'd spent way too much time in self-reflection and learned a lot. Now I could see as plain as the nose on my face – God hadn't been there for me all those years like I'd always thought. Because who could be that cruel? I'd been a faithful wife to a ghost who'd been two-timing me the whole time! Almost everyone I loved died at about the same time! My son bailed on me the first chance he got!

No, it was too much. For years, each new disastrous thing to happen in my life had cut another string. Snip, snip. The waves around me had gotten larger. The storm over me had gotten stronger. With no help, no savior in sight. I was always alone on a road to nowhere.

The only tiny little thread I had clung to was my son, Paul. Yet, in the end, he'd yanked that connection so hard I was sure it was gone as well. His anger so palpable when we'd had that fight about his father. My body still hurt remembering his words hitting me like a battering ram: "liar!" I should've responded to his questions, told him why I'd never said anything about Tom. Instead, I'd hung my head in shame and accepted the blame for Tom's failing as if they were my own.

If a link still existed between my child and I, it was thinner than a spider's silk and just as translucent. After all, he'd texted but the once since I'd fled to come here. Leaving me with little doubt that there was nothing to do but allow my child the space he needed to heal. I'd wounded him with my words and anger.

Oh, I know, one day it more than likely would be me who'd be the one to tell him the horrible truth about his father. As much as it pained me to imagine having to say the words, I would still have to do it. I would still have to say, "Your father married two women at the same time. Your father didn't choose you when you were a baby."

Because, there wasn't a snowball's chance in heck Tom or Stella would ever be honest about what their relationship was. This burden was mine, knowing the truth and being the sanest one in the mix. Yet, I had no idea when or if the time would ever be right for such a conversation with Paul. And I so didn't want to say a word until he was ready.

For my own sanity, I chucked it all in. And ran. It was the best thing I'd ever managed to do in my life. Something I should've found the courage to do the day after I got married. You can say I'm a coward. Me? I think I'd seen too much, done too much, had too many people look down on me for daring to breathe. I needed the space to find a way back to me if I'd ever been me in the first place.

Because people pushed me around my whole life. First, I'd been the good little girl who did what her parents told her to do. Then I'd been the good Christian girl and wife who did what the church told her to do. Finally, I'd tried to be the good mother the world told her to be. But I don't think any of those three were me. Now was my time, if I could find a safe shore to put my feet on. I needed to learn how to stand. I needed to find the right path for me, the real way to find peace. Not follow the road everyone said I should walk on.

Yet moving didn't seem to have helped much. As I cried, the water was drowning me. But for once in my life, someone knew my truth. All of those little pebbles of doubt and pain I'd used to build the walls around my heart had now washed away in my flood of tears. And in my mind, it seemed like they were building a bridge to somewhere. Nevertheless, my child felt farther away than ever.

Chapter 20

Breathing in a deep, cleansing breath, I looked around at Hank and Jessie. Both now sat next to me on the floor, each holding one of my hands.

"Uhm, you guys okay? You're not mad at me?" I squeezed their hands. "I'm a train wreck. Best get out while the getting is good. My own child didn't want to be anywhere near me."

"I think people mistreated you for no reason. Happens to me too. And now I understand why you didn't want a second date; you want to focus on getting your son back. I'm a distraction. I totally get that." The frown lines on Jessie's dark face softened as he tilted his head away from the light. "But here's what I think needs to happen. You need more than Hank's help with this little project of yours. Not because you two can't handle it, but because you need to see all of the people who've been praying for you."

I cringed; he hadn't gotten my point. Church people don't help. They stab you in the back while smiling to your face. However, a little part of me screamed, *Amy, you helped everyone and never asked for anything in return. Maybe now it's your turn!*

I worked the inside of my lip with my teeth, trying to frame any kind of response, but I came up empty.

"I understand, Amy. Trust is earned, not given," Jessie whispered as he pushed himself off the floor. "Everything's going to work out just fine; you'll see."

Still unable to form words, I watched as the two of them strode toward the door. As they left, I sensed they were a part of my life now. Not until I finished this house, but for as long as I lived. A connection linked us, slim as it might be.

Hank didn't come back the next day, which was beyond odd. No word of explanation, nothing. He was gone. That night, I fell into a troubled sleep, tossing and turning in the sweltering heat.

The sound of machinery woke me in the morning. Was that a generator and a lawnmower? What's going on? Since neither of the houses on either side of me showed signs of occupation, I'd never once seen anyone around.

Pulling on some shorts and a t-shirt, I emerged from my shed to discover a horde of people all over my property. The tall grass and weeds were almost gone. A boy with a mower was making the final pass or two. A generator sat beside the house with cords running every which way. Someone was doing their best to pressure wash the siding. Someone else was cutting lumber. Pipes and electrical supplies were strewn everywhere.

Standing there watching the hive of activity, I leaned my head on the jam. And sobbed.

I didn't know a single one of these people, yet here they were early on a Saturday morning. Hank came into my water-logged view, giving me a thumbs-up sign as he continued with whatever task he was up to.

Then Jessie sauntered by, a few boards on his broad shoulders. He juggled them as he gave me a quick wave and a salute. Then blew me a kiss.

"What the world needs now is love, sweet love. No, not just for some, but for everyone." The notes of this rang in my head with a new meaning.

God hadn't forsaken me like I'd thought. Love was for even me. I'd been so compassionate to others all these years, yet never allowed myself to point that inward. The person I'd been hardest on was myself.

Because I'd been the problem all along. I'd slipped to the bottom of the hill because of my sins and found myself in a deep dark cave. No, that's not quite right. I'd been seeing everything in the light of living up to the standard of man, not the standard of God. Thus, I'd rejected a whole lot of good things in my life. And kept a bunch of things which I never should've. Yet God should've been enough. I never should've doubted that at all, ever.

From the moment I set foot in this town, God tried to tell me He was still here for me. The nice bus driver helping me when I was so out of sorts the day of my arrival. The odd man who left all of those tools as gifts since he didn't need them anymore. Hank showing up to provide a helping hand and a listening ear. Other things as well, I'm sure.

Yes, here in this place, God had given me a brand-new set of strings to link me to a new life. Didn't matter who these people were. If I was willing to stretch myself out and grab a few of these connections, they'd pull me to shore. Safety and sanity were within my reach for the first time in my life. A whole new set of options were available to me, laid out before me, inviting me to do more than float along as I'd done my whole life.

There were friends who wouldn't judge me for not being what they expected me to be. There was even the opportunity to go out on a date or two and perhaps find myself joined with a partner for all the right reasons this time. No more sliding into marriage because it was expected of me. Here, in this city, I could become whomever I wanted to be. I'd learn to be passionate about myself and what I wanted, for a change. But most important, I could stop judging myself by someone else's standard. I'd been doing that for far too long. Turns out, what I thought was real might not have been all along.

And I was going to make the most of this second chance. No more regrets. No more what-ifs. No more should've beens. Because today was all I had. No more wasting the gifts God had given me.

A taxi pulled to the curb; my eyes were drawn to the bright yellow flash of color. My identical image stepped out, Paul. Without questioning at all the why of my son being here, I smiled and wiped my tears. My heart sang as I took a hesitant step toward him. Forgiveness and healing were possible. Everything was clear now – God provided all I needed at the exact right moment.

Always had and always will.

Thanks for reading. If you have five minutes, you'd make this writer very happy if you could write a short review on Amazon!

https://www.amazon.com/review/create-review?&asin=B09J44YR1M

Or this code will take you right to the page:

ACKNOWLEDGMENTS

A huge thanks to my editors. You understood what I needed, how to make my work stronger and how to push me as a writer. Without you this novel just wouldn't have been the same.

And of course, to all of my beta readers, launch team members, friends, family and other supporters – thanks for making this journey never be a lonely one.

Made in the USA
Columbia, SC
14 April 2023